THE HARMONIUM *in* NORTH INDIAN MUSIC

This book seeks to understand the complex history of the harmonium in North India, analyse the apparent conflict between musical theory and practice, and describe how the instrument is used in musical practice. Is the harmonium an instrument suitable for Indian music? Can it live up to the requirements of Indian music? These questions pervade the whole book, at the end of which, they appear in a whole new light.

The Harmonium *in* North Indian Music

Birgit Abels

New Age Books

THE HARMONIUM IN NORTH INDIAN MUSIC

ISBN: 978-81-7822-309-4

First Indian Edition: Delhi, 2010

Published by
NEW AGE BOOKS
A-44, Naraina Industrial Area, Phase-I
New Delhi 110 028 (INDIA)
Email: nab@vsnl.in
Website: www.newagebooksindia.com

Printed in India
at Shri Jainendra Press
A-45, Naraina Phase-I, New Delhi 110 028

Contents

Acknowledgements

I wish to express my gratitude to all my interlocutors in India, who took the time to sit with me and talk "things harmonium" over. I have included their names in the appendix. Preparatory work for this study was done during research in North India, generously funded by the German Academic Exchange Service (GAES). I am very grateful for their support. I would also like to acknowledge the International Institute for Asian Studies (IIAS) in Leiden and the University of Amsterdam, Netherlands, for providing generous arrangements and space through a research fellowship, during which the final editing of this book was done.

Christian Ahrens, Ruhr University Bochum (Germany), inspired this book, and it would certainly not have been written without his mentorship and guidance. I owe you. Jonas Braasch, now at the Rensselaer Polytechnic Institute in Troy, NY (USA), did some of the acoustical analyses that have been included in the appendix; for this, my sincere thanks. Johan Malan very carefully translated the bulk of the manuscript, which was originally written in German. I am grateful to Wim van der Meer for providing important information. Finally, I would like to thank Joep Bor for his insights, his mind-boggling knowledge of sources and his constructive critique.

List of Illustrations

I

Introduction

In the sphere of Indian classical music, hardly any instrument offers as much potential for dispute as the harmonium: it is unable to be tuned "properly", ornaments essential for the performance of *ragas* are beyond its capabilities, and it is an imported instrument, an aspect, however, which has lost its significance over the years. Yet the majority of vocalists using the harmonium for melodic accompaniment shrug off these arguments, put forward by those who reject the harmonium. The harmonium's decisive advantages for musicians lie in the specific, vocal-like timbre of the free reeds, its volume, and especially its practicality: contrary to the *sarangi* no extensive tuning is required, the tuning is robust enough to withstand any changes of climate, it is easily transportable and can adapt to the singer's voice to a certain degree.

There is, however, general disagreement on whether Indian music can be performed on the instrument, and public interest in the debate is accordingly intense, as the controversially written articles and discussions in newspapers prove to this day. The matter has evaded scientific scrutiny until now,[1] apart from a few magazine articles – surprisingly insofar as the subject displays many facets and touches on core issues of Indian music: the tuning issue, the definition of the *raga*, the importance of ornamentation and the relationship between Indian classical music and musical change in India. An investigation of the harmonium in India could therefore throw light upon aspects of these important issues.

Because an investigation of the harmonium touches upon basic principles of the Indian musical system, this study will also investigate musical and social aspects concerning the harmonium; technical details comparing the Indian harmonium to its European counterparts and ancestors will mostly stay in the background.

Furthermore, this investigation focuses on "North Indian classical music" in a broad sense. This geographic limitation of the subject takes into account the fact that southern India has an independent and autonomous musical system, an investigation of which would go beyond the scope of this study. "Classical" means that the classical and semi-classical genres of *khyal* and *thumri* (and, in passing, *ghazal*) are the subjects of examination – these are the genres relying heavily on the use of the harmonium, and they are also subject to fundamental theoretical-qualitative postulates of classical music. The harmonium, therefore, assumes a particularly controversial role within these genres, making them all the more interesting as a focal point for an investigation of this kind.

The central question this publication seeks to answer is why, of all instruments, the harmonium managed to proliferate this way, making it indispensable to the modern music and concert scene. This study is divided into two sections: the first is historical in nature, looking at the spread of the harmonium in India and analysing the dispute between the harmonium's advocates and their opponents within their context.

This first part examines primary and secondary sources, historic recordings and information gathered during field research in India. The latter is also examined in the second section, which analyses the musical role the harmonium plays.

The harmonium is also played as a solo instrument, but this genre is largely an area of research in itself, and can only be looked at cursorily. It is a genre with a low profile in current public concert life, therefore this limitation does not distort the investigation.

The analysis of the harmonium's accompaniment function looks at strategies that musicians apply to compensate for the acknowledged limitations of their instrument. Closely related to this is the question of how the role of a melodic instrument accompanying a singer is defined, which has been investigated (albeit not published)[2] and to which this publication provides a few additional answers.

Endnotes

1. The only thesis written on the topic is unpublished: John Napier, *The Introduction and Use of the Harmonium in North Indian Classical Music*, M.A. thesis (Ms) Sydney: University of New South Wales 1994. Other authors, however, have in various contexts touched upon the issue, including Joep Bor, Jonas Braasch & Gregor Klinke, Bigamudre Chaitanya Deva, Gerry Farrell, Neil Sorrell, Peter Manuel (see bibliography for details).
2. John Napier, *Sangat: Melodic Accompaniment in North Indian Vocal Music*, 2 volumes, PhD thesis (Ms) Sydney: University of New South Wales 2001.

II

History of the Harmonium in India

II.1 EARLY HISTORY UNTIL 1884

With the current state of knowledge, any attempt to specify when, how and in which form the harmonium became established in India is futile. Literature states anything between the end of the 18th century[1] – which is *de facto* impossible, since the harmonium was only patented in the middle of the 19th century – and the middle of the 19th century. There are too few sources to enable a complete chronological documentation on the history of the harmonium in India. Therefore, I use several systematic approaches to the issue in order to shed light on it from different perspectives.

II.1.1 The Cultural-Historical Context

The first known mention of the harmonium in Indian literature dates back from 1868.[2] Assuming the import of a fully developed European harmonium, the earliest possible date could be the early 1840s, since Alexandre Debain patented his (pressure system) harmonium in 1842, and none of the many parallel developments could have been exported much earlier. The idea of an indigenous Indian development can be abandoned: although the free reed principle is a South-East-

Asian development and its manufacture in Europe a reaction to knowledge of the corresponding instruments[3], this type of reed played no veritable role in India at the time.

What seems to be another "novelty" for Indian instrument manufacture – the keyboard – is a different case. Independently from the not yet entirely explored use of keyed instruments within the context of proselytisation, they had a certain representative function as diplomatic gifts. In 1579, an organ was presented at the court of Akbar in Fatehpur Sikri, and organ music played a certain role at the Mogul's court during the following decades.[4] These European instruments, becoming highly symbolical objects of prestige, initially had a neutral function of cultural ambassadorship, starting with the onset of European presence in India.

A close relationship between musical instrument and cultural identity is evident in the situation the first British settlers were faced with in the Indian colonies: they were a small minority of great affluence, only starting to appreciate the cultural past and present of India, and accordingly seeing themselves faced with an "Other". Domestic musical education and practice boomed accordingly in the European households of the first British settlements.[5]

This situation fostered an environment that even much later, in the mid-19th century, was favourable not only for the harmonium, but for all types of European instruments. Yet when something new was developed in the field of instrument making (as was the case with the harmonium at the time), another psychological aspect comes into play:

> The need to keep up with London fashion, for example, was an important element in the psyche of Calcutta's European residents, and this fuelled a constant demand for the latest fashions, in pianofortes as much as in dresses.[6]

The further away the country of origin was and the more difficult it was to obtain the coveted object, the more prestigious the "latest craze" became. It seems obvious that this frame of mind, borne entirely by non-musical aspects, led to an extraordinarily open-minded attitude towards innovations, making it easy for a new instrument like the harmonium to gain a foothold. As an alternative to the piano, the harpsichord and other common European instruments suitable for soloistic domestic performance, the harmonium offered a decisive advantage: stringed instruments certainly were problematic export goods, since the fragile and tightly fitting woodwork showed little tolerance for the abrupt change of climate and high humidity. In addition, termites posed a real threat to wooden piano frames at that time, as piano builders' attempts to create instruments suitable for the tropics had not yet yielded any satisfying results. Nevertheless, the pianoforte remained a status symbol with a function within the British households that was not to be relinquished easily. Still, instruments with free reeds could be used as substitutes, being more robust and therefore offering a long-term alternative to the piano, also for musical purposes.[7] And even if the abrupt change of climate had an effect on the harmonium's tuning, it was much less severe than with the piano.

In academic literature, the possibility that the harmonium's introduction to India could have been outside the context of Christian proselytisation is hardly considered.[8] The harmonium gained a firm foothold early on and in many missionary stations – for want of a church organ the harmonium presented an alternative for several reasons: its tuning was robust, it was comparatively easy to transport, and no calcants were required – for all these reasons it was most suitable for Christian music. But from a historical viewpoint, one cannot assume that the missionaries brought along harmoniums from the start:[9] the missionaries were sent out before the harmonium was developed, which means that the instrument's establishment must have been brought about by some directive from the mission headquarters. This could not be substantiated yet. Independently from that, it is also possible that diverse keyed instruments (e.g. portative organs) were assumed to be harmoniums at a later stage, which may have contributed to the association of the harmonium with Christian missions.

What can be verified is the import of many instruments for a different purpose, namely for domestic performance in the European households in India (as mentioned earlier), especially in Calcutta (Kolkata).[10] Jotindra Mohan Tagore (born 1831) is said to have imported the first musical boxes and barrel organs,[11] but it most likely means that he was the first Indian to import these instruments.

By the 1880s, the import figures for harmoniums had increased impressively – initially the instruments were imported from Britain, later also from the USA. It seems that by that time, a local harmonium manufacture had already taken shape: in his *Gita Sutra Sar* of 1885-86, Krishna Dhan Banerjee speaks of tuning issues typical for "the country-made harmoniums that have become ubiquitous in India".[12] The main reason for this rise of a local harmonium manufacture was probably that the "bulky pedal Harmonium manufactured by Alexandre and other French makers were expensive and unsuitable for the average Indian homes".[13] Nonetheless, the occasional import of European musical instruments that had begun some decades earlier developed into an independent branch of trade,[14] which no longer (as opposed to the apparent situation before that) was firmly in British hands, but offered British, Anglo-Indians (Indians with Anglophone education) and Indians an opportunity to do business to an equal extent. Dwarkin & Son Ltd. is one of the firms that thrived dealing with imported instruments. When the company was founded in 1875, the harmonium – which, apart from organs, was its most important merchandise – was already common. These instruments imported from Anglophone countries were also sold to missionaries, but primarily to the 'elites of Indian homes'.[15] What is meant is firstly the families of the British Raj, *i. e.* European households of the upper social class, but also (especially as far as the Kolkata firms are concerned) members of the *Brahmo Samaj*, the reformist-religious society situated in Bengal whose progressive members mainly cultivated European thought and culture. The *Brahmo Samaj* used the harmonium to accompany songs at religious meetings and to perform Western music privately. The history and formation of the Bengal middle class (as it is often called and to which the *Brahmo Samaj* belongs) is a phenomenon of social history that has been described often,[16] and this group can be seen as a second link between British and Indian circles, along with the missionaries. The *Brahmo Samaj* seems to be one of the first institution-like Indian circles that adopted the harmonium.[17] This corelates with the fundamentally progressive attitude of the society, an attitude also extremely open towards the 'West', and which was accompanied by the patronage of indigenous musical traditions and the cultivation of Sanskrit poetry as well as the study of traditional local music[18] and European concert music[19] with equal open-mindedness, not only in the *Samaj* households. It seems that on the European side the separation was stronger; at home the European tradition tended to be practised, and Europeans only acted as patrons of indigenous artists within the context of public gatherings with a political nature[20], or when they were interested in the "Orient".[21]

An indispensable prerequisite for the formation of a cultural group such as the Bengali Renaissance[22] is the kind of patronage that had become rarer after the disintegration of the Mogul empire and could only be exercised by the *nawabs* and wealthy families like the Tagores.[23] That the financial *status quo* of affluent families (especially in Bengal) was mostly based on contacts with the East India Company (again, the Tagores are a prime example[24]) shows that this development also occurred in the sphere of European influence.

The British Raj installed itself at a time of total upheaval: between the declining Mogul empire, an uncertain future and the increasing European presence. For certain social groups (including the Bengali Renaissance), the situation emphasised the need to locate the Own position on the changing cultural map of India: between two main poles, in a conflict where it seemed highly urgent to define one's Own place. The need for reforms (culturally as well as institutionally) was beyond dispute in these circles, but the opinion that the European model could not offer a quick alternative and indeed was a destructive force took some time to become popular. "While traditional culture appeared inadequate to meet the challenge posed by the west, colonial hegemonisation tended to destroy the tradition itself"[25] – which inevitably resulted in a critical stance towards both.

This Janus-faced relationship with British cultural hegemony prompted Sourindro Mohan Tagore to state during a lecture in 1870:

> India has been under British rule for a long time and has learned many things from her, but does her music still satisfy us? […] O, Mother India!!! It is a sad fact that in this year of 1870, while many arts and sciences are being discussed indicating the advancement of civilization, we still see none of your offspring attempting to improve the national music.[26]

Tagore's patronage of classical Indian music was by all means ideologically motivated and almost a kind of "national concern" for some. This notion of India's musical potential, as something to be conserved and guided to new horizons, was nothing new at this time: according to Charles Capwell's description, Sourindro Tagore's grandfather already had a reformist "desire to raise the status of Indian music".[27] This basic disposition for innovation has refunctionalised the Own tradition to a vehicle for modernisation. This fundamental willingness for renewal was a prerequisite for the "privatisation" of cultural patronage, and was a consequence of the exposure to the different, apparently superior, British culture. This phenomenon had its most direct effect on culture and education:

> Resurrection of the past, identification of modernity in tradition, an enquiry to establish the superiority of traditional knowledge and achievements [...] were the chief characteristics of this response. [...] The areas in which the colonial cultural enterprise met with immediate reaction were religion, language and education.[28]

Martin Stokes mainly refers to the modern Diaspora when he writes: "[...] Music is socially meaningful not entirely, but largely, because it provides a means by which people recognise identities and places, and the boundaries which separate them",[29] but the same is valid for the early colonial period, and not only in India. This abstraction nevertheless suggests a static character, which cannot be said of the realities referred to. "Identity" in Stokes' sense is inevitably dynamic and interacts in opposition to, conformity with and dependency on the different cultural strands and – within the colonial context – the colonial culture. In the case of India – or more concretely, Bengal – this disposition to see the future differently remained an elitist phenomenon, also with regard to its effect on the performance of classical music (such as the establishment of "orchestral music", see below); which comes as no surprise, seeing that the performance of music (like the possibility of occupying oneself with European thought, initially) had been an exclusive privilege for generations.

II.1.2 The Spatial Context

Apart from the long process of political change, the concrete local prerequisites for the described development are of an economical and intellectual nature. Kolkata, the centre of British presence with educational institutions like Fort William College[30] (which was founded in 1800 to educate 'young civil servants' for the East India Company), presents a special case. In 1816, Hindu College was founded here, too. The close vicinity of these centres of learning created a fertile environment in which the Own and the Other culture were exposed to each other to some degree, and naturally resulted in the most diverse, but reflected positions; it is not without reason that many of the early strands of the independence movement can be traced back to greater Kolkata.

The intellectual climate developing in the 19th century created such a favourable situation for the novel harmonium (which was as new to the Europeans as it was to the Indians) in Kolkata that the city remains the centre of harmonium manufacture in India to this day.

Sources on the subject are rare, and in Bengal it is usually the same circle of persons whose musical activities can be verified at all: especially the Tagore family and its direct proximity.

At least one Tagore household had an organ as well as a harmonium,[31] which were used for composition and the like in the sons' (cousins of Rabindranath) Anglophone and European-influenced education. One of these sons, Sourindro Mohan Tagore (1840–1914) is ascribed an important role in spreading the harmonium.[32] Taking into account his birth date and that the same source states that especially his brother Jotindro occupied himself with the harmonium intensively, one can assume that a harmonium must have been in the household in the early 1850s, or at the latest by the mid-1850s. It probably was a European model, similar to the one in Fig. 1.

P. Banerjea also credits Jotindro with promoting the harmonium in connection with 'orchestral music' as early as the late 1860s:

Fig. 1: An undated illustration of a courtesan playing a harmonium of European design used in India.

> [...] but it is Maharaja Jotindra Mohan Tagore who, with the valuable assistance of the venerable Professor Kshetra Mohan Goswami, has introduced the so-called *concert* into Bengal. The orchestral music was first practised about 20 years ago, in the Belgachia garden of Raja Pratap Chandra Singh of Paikpara, at the time of the performance of the *Ratnabali Natak* [...] The musical instruments commonly used in an orchestral party are – one harmonium, a pair of *Behalas* or violins, a pair of tenors, a pair of flutes, one clarionet, one violoncello, one double base, one *Mridanga*, and a pair of *Karatals*.[33]

In Sourindro Mohan Tagore's *Universal History of Music*, Jotindro was associated with Bengali theatre music:

> The first Bengali amateur theatre was started in 1858 at the Belgatchia Villa of Rajah Pratap Narain Singh of Paikpara in the suburbs of Calcutta, under the supervision of some of the prominent members of the educated Hindu society of Calcutta. Maharahjah Bahadur Sir Jotindro Mohan Tagore, K.C.S.I., took an active part in its get-up, and composed for the orchestra organised for it a few airs [sic] which are the first of their kind. This orchestra consisted mostly of European instruments.[34]

These 'European instruments' in all likelihood included one or several harmoniums. Most interestingly, S.M. Tagore adds that the instrumentation of these orchestras changed:

> Later on, when theatricals began annually to be given at the Maharaja's family residence in Pathuriaghatta Street, Calcutta, the orchestra was made up entirely of

> Indian instruments, and most of the airs played in it were composed by the author of this publication [*i.e.*, Sourindro Mohan Tagore]. Some professional theatres have, within the last 25 years, been set up in Calcutta in most of whose orchestras Hindu music is played on European instruments.[35]

Sourindro later founded music schools modelled on European examples (in which an Indian musical notation was used, because he regarded the European notation as not universally appropriate), and if one considers the fact that he must have written the *Harmonium Sutra* before 1881 (see note 4), he must have had the required attitude towards the instrument as well as the suitable infrastructure (the music schools) to propagate the instrument by then.

But Bengal is not the only area that seems to play an important role in the early history of the harmonium in India. If some clues lead to Bengali theatre, the local theatre variants in Maharashtra also appeared comparatively early in connection with the harmonium. Here the theatre was of great significance.[36] The ensembles were mostly travelling theatre troupes, performing diverse classical plays translated from Sanskrit, for example; later several plays by Shakespeare were performed too.[37] Two characteristics distinguish the Marathi theatre from other local theatres: the troupes operated on relatively small budgets, and in the sub-genre 'sangeet dramas' they displayed an "excessive love of songs and constant repetitions"[38]– both features that make the use of a harmonium seem reasonable by all means.

Traditionally the numerous "songs" in the Marathi-plays were accompanied by *tabla, sarangi* and two *tanpuras*, the latter placed on either side of the stage and providing a musical frame (they were not even visible from the first row in the audience).[39]

The titles were taken from the most diverse genres, depending on the choice of musician; it ranged from folk songs to the *khyal* repertoire, mostly semi-classical in nature. This was another factor that facilitated the harmonium's establishment: the repertoire "was not rigorously classical, it did not have to adhere in too meticulous a manner to *raga* structures",[40] which means the use of an instrument like the harmonium created no serious problem in this regard. Even if the essentialist nature of this phrase does no justice to the diversity and the quite independent sub-groups of the Marathi genre, it still means that there was a level of flexibility – especially concerning *shrutis* and other musical subtleties – that was indispensable for the harmonium to gain a foothold.

According to earlier research the (pedal-) harmonium appeared on the Marathi stage around 1882,[41] on the initiative of Annasahib Kirloskar (1843–1885), author and director of numerous theatre pieces.[42] Until then the musicians were placed at the sides of the stage, but with the appearance of the harmonium (or "organ"[43]) the European arrangement was adapted: the instrument now stood in front of the stage in an orchestra pit of sorts, while two smaller instruments were placed on either side of the stage; later two *sarangis* were added. A percussionist (usually a *tabla*-player) always was included in the ensemble.[44] Ashok Ranade assumes that this was done to accommodate the obviously stronger voices of the young singers.[45] But it is more likely that the growing audiences meant larger halls, demanding a higher volume level. This combination of instruments for accompaniment was unique in size at the time, and only reappeared at the end of the 20th century in *ghazal*'s orchestral, Europe-oriented instrumentation. With it the nature of stage accompaniment changed fundamentally, and the employment of up to three harmoniums or similar instruments accompanying melodically meant that the character of the entire genre was transformed. What seems to be decisive is that for the first time (?), so many (up to five) instruments played simultaneously. Dyaneshwar Nadkarni describes the situation as follows:

> When the singer-actor stepped towards the footlights, he got his basic musical cue from the organs. Having established rapport mainly with the central organ and with the *sarangis*, he could sing in the right register. But, because he was dependent on this accompaniment, he rarely left his position [...].[46]

Once the harmonium was adopted by the theatre, the subsequent history can be traced by means of the (somewhat panegyrizing) biographies of single persons. Govindrao Tembe

Fig. 2: A pedal harmonium, equipped with resonators for theatre use.

(1881–1955), at some point a member of Bal Gandharva's theatre troupe Gandharva Natak Mandali,[47] played an important role. He has often been described as a dazzling figure in the history of the Marathi theatre as well as the Indian harmonium.[48] Tembe, largely an autodidact as far as the harmonium is concerned, also selected the musical numbers for plays.[49] 20th century Indian musicological literature makes a clear judgement, which one can assume only reappeared recently: "Perhaps because the harmonium could not fully absorb Govindrao's musical virtuosity, the overflow was diverted to theatre."[50] Today Tembe's name summons up the association Marathi-theatre-harmonium.

From a musical perspective, the Marathi theatre's most prominent characteristic was its stylistic flexibility (especially at this early stage) which did not simply lead to an eclectic mixture of styles, but contributed to the development of the individual styles.

All this took place within close proximity of the classical music scene, for the audience seems to have been largely overlapping. Especially *thumri* and *khyal* were influenced by the mentioned flexibility. This made the Marathi stage a breeding ground for musical innovation and new ideas, which – because at the same time the performance conformed largely to the norms of the tradition and the genres – managed to have an influence on classical music beyond the stage.[51]

Thus the harmonium found its way into the musical culture of the cities and colonial centres in North India; yet the actual spread took place in rural areas, in a musical context in which social aspects (because of the low level of European presence) played a different role than in urban areas. From the point onwards when the harmonium advanced from a status symbol for wealthy families to an instrument of the people's theatre, prestige and European origin still played a role, but it was placed in an entirely different context: it was 'Indianised'.

II.1.3 The Spreading of The Harmonium

The interaction between theatre music and non-theatre music was mutual with regard to *thumri*, seeing that the musicians' training naturally did not differentiate between theatre music and non-theatre music. Bhaya Sahib Ganpat Rao (1852–1920) is said to have established the harmonium as a standard accompanying instrument in this genre[52] – with parallel *sarangi* accompaniment and without. Several of his students played an important role in the further spreading of the instrument: the famous Gauhar Jan, one of his students, was among the first to record with harmonium accompaniment;[53] another disciple Sohan Singh (1874-1931)[54] "grew into a noted Thumri singer and an excellent Harmonium player";[55] Bashir Khan, who died in 1938, became a "fine Harmonium player"[56] under his tutelage; and Mirza Saheb of Lucknow was also considered "a great Harmonium player".[57]

It is interesting that by all evidence, *thumri* was among the first genres in which the harmonium was embraced: *thumri* singers were often accompanied and trained by *sarangi* players, making the *sarangi* players the core of the genre. Up to the 1960s, *thumri* singers were taught, as far as possible, by *sarangi* players[58], and music accompanied by *sarangi* only (without harmonium) or with both instruments was more common in this repertoire than in *khyal*.

In tracing the relationship between *thumri* and other musical genres, the harmonium's path into the "big" genre of *khyal* comes to light. The aforementioned Bhaya Sahib Rao, who was extremely influential[59] in spreading the harmonium, was a son of the maharaja Jayaji Rao Scindia of Gwalior and a well-known singer,[60] and he came from the direct vicinity of the Gwalior *gharana*, which was the school (even before the Jaipur *gharana*) with the earliest and closest ties to the theatre.[61]

Amal Das Sharma and John Napier have described the network structure of Bhaya Sahib's *gharana*-spanning learning and teaching relationships, over which he could propagate the harmonium at an amazing rate.[62]

Thus it seems that by around 1900, the harmonium established itself as a common instrument associated with the 'lighter' genres like *thumri*, *ghazal*, and also *dadra*.[63] The repertoire of *thumri* singers usually spans several genres, also *khyal*, so that the inspiration by the development in one genre could influence another. One notable aspect of the harmonium's adoption across musical genres is the fact that this process excluded the transfer of other features – even though many women played[64] and propagated the harmonium in *thumri*, the male dominance in *khyal* persisted at this time. Manuel notes that many of these *khyal* singers grew up[65] in the courtesan environment, *i.e.* they came from families whose male members had the responsibility of training courtesans musically and accompanying them on the *sarangi*.

The 'young' generation at the turn of the century (of which many musicians abandoned the *sarangi* to become singers) displayed 'feminisms' in their vocal technique that can be traced back directly to the courtesan style.[66] It is striking that many of the harmonium's early protégés among *khyal*-singers had a more or less strong feminine nuance for the time: Abdul Karim Khan (1882–1937), one of the first *khyal* singers to integrate the harmonium into his ensemble, is known for his strongly nasal singing technique. Apart from that he cultivated a "sweet voice".[67] Pyara Sahib and Anant Nath Bose were firstly *thumri* singers, but they sang falsetto and in addition consciously tried to imitate the gestures and vocal intonation of the courtesans.[68] An erotic effect may have been intended in playing with the gender roles.

Between the somewhat effeminate vocal technique and the adoption of the harmonium I see a connection: Even if the *sarangi* is still[69] regarded as the instrument 'theoretically' most suitable to accompany the human voice, the harmonium today offers a much better alternative for many musicians, solely in terms of tonal colour. The arguments used most often in this context are a certain timbral softness and the possibility to blend the instrumental and the vocal sound through the appropriate selection of reeds. The ideal is to arrive at a blend of voice and accompanying instrument – which, in my opinion, is easier to obtain with a free reed instrument[70] than with a bowed instrument, especially in the high register. The discovery of this affinity between reed and vocal timbre most likely was the prime motivation for high register singers to use and establish the harmonium as an accompanying instrument, as is said of Abdul Karim Khan, although Krishna Dhan Banerjee states that at least locally built harmoniums at the time "generally injure[d] the sweetness of the voice" due to the "formation of frequent beats", *i.e.* bad tuning.[71] This, however, is a problem that he limits to Indian-built harmoniums: by contrast, harmoniums "being imports from Europe, and generally of good make, were mostly sweetly sounding".[72] It is therefore not surprising that in the above-mentioned group a relatively high number of "harmonium pioneers" can be found.

The harmonium spread very fast. Whether high or low voice, it is striking that many singers from this social background and with connections to the courtesan milieu were protégés of the harmonium, and this regardless of genre. In addition to the musical aspect, the sociological perspective again offers an approach: In the 19th century, there was an "upward mobility" among the *sarangi* players, *i.e.* many musicians became more aware of their own musical skills as compared to the vocal soloists' skills; the option of becoming a vocal soloist became much more common, while providing *sarangi* accompaniment moved to the background.[73]

In the literature on the topic there is one constantly recurring topos: that the *sarangi* was ousted as *khyal's* accompanying instrument by the harmonium. John Napier does not agree:

> [...] the *sarangi* became the paradigmatic accompanying instrument for *khyal* in the early decades of the twentieth century, though its use in the accompaniment of dance substantially supersedes this. Almost at the same time as it achieved this status, it began to be superseded by the harmonium. The two instruments have competed for the role of accompanying instrument ever since.[74].

The crucial point, Napier goes on, is that in spite of the *sarangi's* clearly acknowledged antiquity the harmonium did not oust the *sarangi* as accompanying instrument, but that when the harmonium appeared in India, the instruments were in the same starting position, both having the potential to become accompanying instruments – a function fulfilled until then primarily by diverse other instruments but not necessarily demanded by the aesthetic ideal. Amir Khan, for instance, is said to have advocated the "pure *khyal*", which needed no instruments other than *tanpura* and *tabla*[75] – and that regardless of the fact that he stemmed from a family that earned a living playing the *sarangi*, also in his generation.[76] The *sarangi*, therefore, was anything but firmly established by the time competition appeared in the form of the harmonium, Napier conjectures. Drawing on substantial pictorial and textual evidence, Joep Bor, by contrast, holds a different opinion: unlike the harmonium, the *sarangi* had been well established by the mid-18th century as an accompaniment of female singers and by the mid-19th century of male singers, and it was the increasing competition and rivalry between *khyal* singers and *sarangi* accompanists that opened the door through which the harmonium came in.[77] In both theories, the same theme plays a decisive role: the competition between the musicians.

In addition to the musically inherent requirements of the accompaniment, the fact that the venues that had to be filled with sound grew larger (due to social change and new technology, such as the microphone, especially) plays a role that should not be underestimated. In terms of sound volume the harmonium clearly has an advantage over the *sarangi* when compared directly. Other reasons for the *sarangi's* "demise" have been described in detail by Joep Bor,[78] who also relates these reasons to the harmonium: the *sarangi* had the "disadvantage" of being firmly connected with a strong stigmatisation.

From a musical point of view, most likely one mundane reason made the *sarangi* less attractive: tuning the instrument usually takes several minutes and the result depends entirely on the ear of the player, who tunes his instrument himself. Today the vocalist, and only he or she, not the *tanpura* player himself or herself, is supposed to tune the *tanpura*, even if sometimes it is only to demonstrate the hierarchical structure.[79] This especially relates to the changed relationship between the "new" soloist and accompanist: the harmonium does not need to be tuned, meaning that the dominance of the singer over the accompanist is not emphasised specifically.

* * *

In Kolkata during the early 19th century "[...] we find a peculiar amalgam of tastes in the cultural behaviour of the members of this first generation of the Bengali elite".[80] This has various meanings: (1) the "Renaissance" of the classical Indian tradition, (2) the cultivation of popular genres[81] within the general framework of classical music as well as 3) the study of European music for whichever reason.[82] This kind of cultural examination, for which the term "cultural schizophrenia"[83] was occasionally used in earlier writings, already assumed considerable proportions in the closing quarter of the 18th century – but was not to lead to the permanent parallel existence of several different cultures: "By the middle of the [19th] century [...] the elements of the folk cultural tradition were to be consciously eschewed".[84] Parallel to the cultivation of the European arts, this caused a promotion of the idea of the "Great Traditions", which by all means seemed to look for commonalities with their European counterparts as far as content was concerned.[85] Turning away from the popular traditions could also, however, lead to the sole cultivation of Indian classical music as a standpoint opposing that of the acquisition of European music culture. This was a musical result of the developing political nationalism. The appearance of this apparently unrelated, ideological moment created a field of tension that was to influence the unfolding discussion regarding the instrument (see Chapter II.2): a field of tension between the art music tradition, the 'folk' music traditions and the British "higher education", all three with various social connotations.

In the course of time, the influence of these aspects soon faded sufficiently for the harmonium to be absorbed into the popular tradition, as well as the theatre. This necessarily had to be preceded by a period of familiarisation in order for the instrument to shed its social connotations and yet appear onstage as a novelty. The instrument could establish itself as soon as it had been present long enough not to be perceived as purely "European" or "British" any more.

Local demand for the harmonium was tried to be met with local sources (see below), but also with collaboration in

Fig. 3: Postcard with the title: 'Colombo Dancing Girl', without date.

instrument manufacture with European harmonium makers. Evidence of this is the instrument shown in Fig. 4. On the white company label (centred on the front side) is written: "Kasriel, Paris – T.S. Ramchunder, Bombay". According to the owners, Phil and Pam Fluke, the instrument was built especially for Ramchunder by Kasriel, or Ramchunder copied or adapted the Kasriel model.[86] The instrument dates back to 1895, *i.e.* a time at which the harmonium was common in India.

The thesis that the instrument was forced upon Indian musicians by Europeans will be proved wrong – especially the "discussion of the discussion" between Indians and Orientalists will bring to light some of the mechanisms at work; the argumentations for and against the harmonium often actually had entirely different aims, aims that were not of musical nature.

Fig. 4: Harmonium of Kasriel/Ramchunder. From the collection of Phil and Pam Fluke, Saltaire.

II.2 AFTER 1884 : THE 'INDIAN' HARMONIUM

The most significant characteristic distinguishing the harmonium from its European counterpart is the fact that the bellows is attached to the back of the instrument, where it is operated with the left hand; because the instrument is intended to be played whilst sitting on the ground, it lacks legs or the corresponding supporting structure. This accommodated the everyday needs of the Indian musician. Technically the European and Indian instruments are largely similar. As far as wind systems are concerned, most Indian instruments are operated with pressure, while there are instruments with vacuum systems.[87] The outward change of appearance had other effects than purely practical ones: because it looked different from the European models, it could emancipate itself from the persistent association with European culture. According to current opinion it became "specifically Indian",[88] and now is "without any role model in Europe".[89] Dwarkanath Ghosh, grandfather of Jnan Prakash Ghosh[90] and founder of the company Dwarkin & Son Ltd. in 1875 in Calcutta, is often accredited with the alteration (which is claimed by and ascribed to many[91]). The company has been involved in harmonium manufacture and instrument trade from the start, and also imported European and American instruments. According to advertising material, Ghosh "invented" the "hand harmonium" in 1884;[92] the company had used the word "harmonium" earlier already. The same document cites the "bulky Pedal Harmonium by Alexander [probably Alexandre & Fils, Paris] and other French makers" as direct predecessors. In the indirect context the author mentions an instrument he obviously is not familiar with: the "Harmonium flute [*i.e.* Harmoniflûte] or Organ Accordian". It probably played a decisive role, even if the details cannot be ascertained today.[93] It is described as an "adoption of the German Accordian and Harmonium". In comparing Fig. 5 and Fig. 6, one can easily see that the instrument must have been a direct inspiration in terms of outer appearance (bellows at the back) as well as range, size

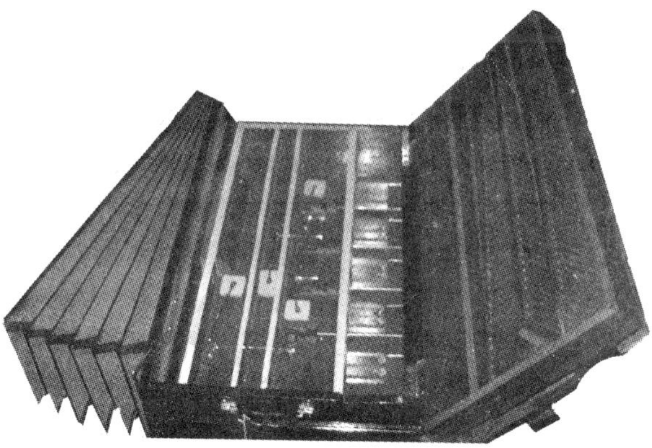

Fig. 5: Indian harmonium with the keyboard lifted to reveal the interior; the bellows is attached to the back of the instrument.

Fig. 6: Harmoniflûte.

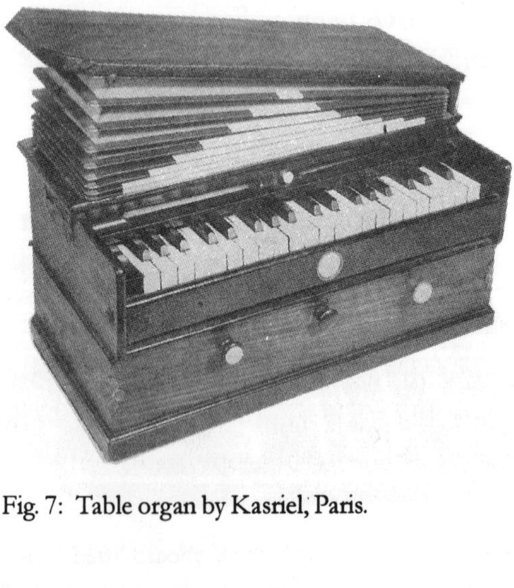

Fig. 7: Table organ by Kasriel, Paris.

Fig. 8: The company BINA still makes pedal harmoniums. Depicted is 'Model No. 21 (Hand & Foot)'

and operation. The fact that this instrument (also known as accordéon-orgue, flûtina, accordéon-flûtina und piano-concertina[94]) obviously was known to the manufacturer who "invented" the Indian harmonium, indicates that Dwarkin & Son traded also with this instrument around the middle of the 19th century and that some of its characteristics went into the development of the "Indian" harmonium.

Excursion: Harmoniflûte

Literature dealing with the harmoniflûte is rare, yet it evokes the suspicion that the instrument's failure to establish itself was due to the same reasons in Europe as in India.

Originally a close relative of the harmonium, it obviously – contrary to the harmonium itself–was sent to India to be used by missionaries:

> Les Harmoniums Kasriel [...] sont de tous types depuis le guide-chant scolaire vant d'utilité publique en vertu d'une instruction ministérielle du 20 juin 1923, en passant par le modèle missionaire pliant, se rentrant dans uns petite caisse contenant les pédales, avec lyre pliante ou montants latéraux également pliants, mais plus simples. Le type de modèle était accommandé pour les chants bengalis ou hindous [sic!]. Ils pouvaient avoir du 31/2 à 4 octaves, et être dotés de 2 à 4 lignes d'anches et d'un nombre important de registres allant jusqu'à 9. Sous cette raison sociale, ont été commercialisés des Harmoniflûtes Busson.[95]

These instruments were made with and without pedals, with pressure and with vacuum systems.[96] Exactly when the harmoniflûte was "invented" still seems to be unclear. Instruments of this type were on display at the World Exhibition of 1867 in Paris, and the exhibition catalogue states: "Les harmoniums, harmonicordes, harmoniflûtes et autres sujets de la méme feuille sont un peu écrasés par le voisinage de pianos"[97]. This merely suggests what Oscar Comettant writes more clearly: that the accordéon-flûte, the harmoniflûte and other instruments "ne savaient s'élever à la dignité d'instruments sérieux."[98]

Fig. 9: Harmoniflûte, built in France between 1850 and 1860.

Therefore the harmoniflûte's fate was sealed at this point in time, in terms of its social connotation and of its use. What might have added to it is that these instruments of delicate construction when compared to the compact and heavy harmoniums, were inexpensive – or cheap; Alexandre-harmoniums in 1897 were sold in France for 700–1000 Francs, while a harmoniflûte could be had for 120 Francs. The phrase: "Le type de modèle était accommandé pour les chants bengalis ou hindous" from the citation above also suggests that the instrument was closely associated with export and proselytisation, an aspect that certainly did not raise its prestige. Fig. 6 paints a different picture, creating the impression that it was an instrument for the drawing room. This could have been the case for a short time, yet it seems to have been a short-lived fashion of the period: the "joy of experimentation and the demand for change" prompted the invention of a plethora of new free reed instruments – to the delight of professionals and laypersons alike[99] – in such quick succession that only a few of these instruments (e.g. the harmonium) could establish itself permanently.

The delicate construction of the harmoniflûte initially was an asset, for the instruments were easily transportable; yet this became a liability, for they were also fragile.[100] This fragility, combined with the fact that the instruments were not suitable for the tropics, meant that the instruments never survived long in the Indian climate.

The main reason, however, for India and Europe alike, why the harmoniflûte failed to establish itself, was another: because of the way the bellows is constructed the sound of the harmoniflûte can not be manipulated, making its dynamics static.[101] That is probably the reason why the instrument never entered musical practice and was only really taken note of retrospectively by academics: "L'Harmoniflûte est un ravissant petit instrument sur pied. Des traces de publicité se rencontrent dans la presse specialisée, assez tardivement. Il a dû avoir du succès."[102]

This handiness of the instrument surely was one of the aspects which made it an example for the "Indian" harmonium to a certain extent. Even if it is impossible to ascertain exactly which alterations Dwarkanath Ghosh (and possibly other instrument makers) made, it seems that the harmoniflûte was the direct precursor of the Indian harmonium, so that it is not a direct descendant of Debain's pedal harmonium.[103]

Without doubt the latter was better known at the time, so that one can assume that Ghosh (and colleagues) looked for ways to modify the harmonium according to Indian requirements, and that the harmoniflûte sparked his imagination. This refers to the outer shape as well as to the bellows system.[104]

This bellows system was subject to a lot of experimentation, and one cannot assume that it was based on one example. The range of the Indian harmonium's manual with its three octaves matches that of the harmoniflûte. Also, the dimensions of the "new" instrument were closer to the harmoniflûte's than to the European harmonium's, which made the instrument easier to transport.

Other instruments could also have served as examples, for instance the table organ depicted in Fig. 7. Thus the Indian harmonium is a hybrid instrument, based at least on these two – albeit related – precursors.

The idea of attaching the bellows to the back of the instrument so that it can be operated with the left hand, ascribed to Dwarkanath Ghosh, therefore obviously was not as free from precursors or European influence or as revolutionary as the literature would like its readers to believe.

But for India it was the decisive idea, and without its application, the rapid spread of the instrument at that time would not have been imaginable.

Apart from this hand-operated model, which is largely similar to the European book harmonium, suitcase harmoniums (simply called "portable harmoniums") are also available.[105] These two types dominate the harmonium market;[106] "dulcetinas" are also built,[107] but only for transportability reasons and in much smaller numbers.[108]

During the same period (1880–1900) the import of harmoniums manufactured in Europe increased sharply. The "tropic models" of the European firms are shaped differently, yet most of them are similar to the book harmonium. If an instrument was declared fit for the tropics, it mainly meant that a special polish[109] was used to protect it from both vermin and high humidity.

The obviously equal use of Indian and European instruments suggests that Ghosh's modification could only have been marginal changes to the outer appearance, compared to the European book and suitcase harmoniums.

Fig. 10: A freed, manufactured in Palitana (Gujarat).

Fig. 11: A set of freeds, manufactured in Palitana (Gujarat).

The inner workings of the different Indian harmonium models are very similar and vary only in details. Generally the instruments are 53–57 cm wide and half as deep. The height differs from model to model, but is usually 3–4 cm less than the depth. The stops are mounted on the front side, and their number is dictated by the configuration of the instrument: the harmonium with the most stops I have seen had twelve. The stops change couplers of all kinds: octave couplers, stop couplers, and others. The so-called *tar* ("feminine") stops can only be used when coupled with the 8' stops (*i.e.* not as a solo stop), therefore serving only as a timbral modifier. Other couplers regulate the wind pressure, raising the volume by increasing the air supply, or set drone pitches (mostly Sa – Pa – Sa – Pa). The latter devices are not part of the "standard configuration", which consists of stop couplers. Couplers are never changed during performance; the timbre selected for the piece is maintained throughout, and is set – for reasons that require investigation later on – to accommodate the singer's vocal timbre during accompaniment.

The reeds are arranged in the wind chest sorted by rank, and mainly differ in pitch: there are, according to the Indian terms used for the three basic octaves, three ranks: *mandra saptak* ("low octave"), *madhya saptak* ("middle octave") and *tar saptak* ("high octave"). The *mandra saptak*-stop of the harmonium is called the bass register, the *madhya saptak*-stop the male and the *tar saptak*-stop the feminine stop. *Madhya saptak* starts around c^1 or d^1, depending on the tonic. Each professional singer has his own harmonium tuned to his personal "tonic", or his accompanist owns a harmonium that is tailored to his voice.[110]

More or less until India's independence in 1947, reed sets of three octaves each were imported from Europe, mainly French and German reeds[111] – this is surprising, regarding the fact that most of the "complete harmoniums" were imported from Great Britain.

"The coming of the war in 1939 appears to have served as the catalyst to encourage local manufacture," reckons Arthur Ord-Hume.[112] This is indeed likely, and after the war the situation in India had changed to such an extent that importing instruments no longer seemed profitable. Harmonium manufacture in Europe also was almost non-existent at the time.

Around the Second World War, the manufacture of reeds commenced in Palitana in the district of Bhavnagar (Gujarat), and the reeds produced here were regarded to be of similar quality to the European reeds; according to local opinion they were "smoother, more suitable for Indian music"[113] than the European reeds. Independently of this timbral aspect, new harmoniums with French or German reeds can be bought to this day, and the use of imported reeds clearly shows in the retail price. In the 1990s, a company in Delhi broke the Palitana-monopoly;[114] for the first time there is economical competition in this field.

Basically, all the necessary parts are manufactured in India. As far as the reeds are concerned, there is no standard alloy used in their manufacture; it is an area of constant experimentation,[115] aiming to create as colourful a timbral palette as possible.

II.3 FOR AND AGAINST THE HARMONIUM: PUBLIC OPINION

II.3.1 The Discussion Until 1940

> "Music" is not only reflexive; it is also generative, both as a cultural system and as human capability, and an important task of musicology is to find out how people make sense of "music" in a variety of social situations and different cultural contexts, and to distinguish between the innate human capabilities that individuals use in the process of making sense of "music" and the cultural conventions that guide their actions.[116]

In these historic lines, Blacking basically summarises the frame of thought of the identity that was manifesting itself musically. The same situation persists within the frame of a transition process, of a mostly subconscious discourse on musical development. If the harmonium's "destructive influence" on Indian music – pars pro toto for innovation, excessive foreign influence and much more – was discussed, it was not only about musical aspects, but at least as much about Blacking's "cultural conventions" and primarily their context. "Making sense of music" was a desideratum for the Indian cultural "upper class", as the quote of Tagore earlier shows. The passion with which the debate unfolded was in my opinion not because a foreign (and musically problematic) instrument appeared on the scene; too early and too easily did the Persian-derived sitar establish itself at an earlier stage, and too simple was the acceptance of the guitar, later on. The discussion's actual background was rather social changes on a higher level, which were directly connected to the intellectual colonialisation.

Before the onset of the colonial period and long thereafter the reflection on the Indian arts was borne by the rigid notion that the art form in question not only had its roots in a great, ancient culture, but also that its current form mirrored this ideal:

> The art music of the present day is a direct descendant of [...] ancient schools, whose traditions have been handed down with comment and expansion in the guilds of the hereditary musicians. [...] India presents to us the wonderful spectacle of the still surviving consciousness of the ancient world [...].[117]

As widely accepted as this notion is, as intangible it is. Which "ancient schools" are meant, and what constitutes the "consciousness of the ancient world" cannot be verified in the sense of historical facts. As far as the theoretical superstructure is concerned, one is mostly referred to a single treatise: Bharata's *Natyashastra*, collated between 200 and 400 AD.[118] There are no references to the implementation of the theoretical, possibly purely prescriptive instructions. Given the size of the Indian subcontinent, the *Natyashastra* could not possibly have had unchangeable, pan-Indian validity. Yet this is exactly what is ascribed to it, and on this basis the common image of that grand, glorious musical culture is created. This ideal is put into relation with the current practice in a two-edged way: initially it legitimates the modern practice by equipping it with a past and with roots in the Vedas, but then it becomes an opposite, in which the modern practice clearly shows the decline of the tradition. The past and present tradition is often used in this context to define the respective counterpart: the past can only be shown this way against the backdrop of such a present, just like the present can only be such a decline of the past ideal. Confronted with the European way of thinking this became a dualistic approach, as Nazir Ali Jairazbhoy explains:

> In much of the writings of Indian authors, one can see a dualistic approach; an attempt to reconcile the values of traditional Indian scholarship with the kind of scholarship which prevails in the West. In traditional Hindu India, the Vedas represent the eternal truth; the world is seen to be in its final period approaching destruction when moral and ethical values are at their lowest ebb. The truth lies in the past. Ancient traditions are revered and early writers generally accepted without question. If present day practice differs from ancient theory, the orthodox view would be to fault the practice and attempt to modify it to conform with the theory. In contrast, the Western approach, which is influencing many writers, tends to set aside moral and ethical considerations in an attempt to be "objective".[119]

This is all based on the clash between the Indian concept of culture – which, contrary to the European attitude, is much more inclined towards consistency than development – and its European counterpart. Jairazbhoy's formulation "dualistic approach" has a negative connotation. From the European perspective it indeed seems remarkable to combine two such contrary approaches, when neither is modifiable. This is basically one of the central points of the entire conflict: is the North Indian musical system tolerant enough to allow changes that can be called "progressive" in European terms, or is the "dignity" of the ancient heritage a bigger responsibility, prohibiting such conscious developments? Which musical elements comprise the identity-generating and timeless part of a musical culture? Without disputing the fact that a modern identity was not possible without an examination of "the Ancient":[120] Which influence must "the Ancient" have, when it is musically so intangible?

As far as the musical facts are concerned, these will be examined in the second part of this book. The next part will be an indirect reflection of the circumstances that led to a conflict that was indirectly carried out in the "arena" of the harmonium,[121] "that bane of Indian music",[122] as Rabindranath Tagore once called it.

Colonialism and "tradition" are two opposing poles between which the discussion in this form becomes possible at all. The harmonium's acceptance was the result of an indirect process of rethinking which – often seemingly disoriented – took place in a triangle of glorious, ancient past, musically inferior present and what seemed to be British superiority. Orientalist interests play as important a role on the British side as cultural acquisition strategies on the Indian side. The dispute nevertheless does not occur along the boundaries of cultural affiliation: both can also be diagnosed vice versa. Some comments can only be understood in the light of an analysis according to Edward Said, which presupposes that "Orient", "Occident" and also "cultural identity" are primarily constructed frames of thought, and that they only secondarily pertain to reality or experience.[123]

Texts are the only sources casting light on the course of the discussion. What is striking about the early European texts on Indian music – those written in the late 18th and early 19th centuries[124] – is the clearly ambivalent perception of Indian culture: on the one hand there is a retrogressive admiration of the country as a hoard of ancient wisdom,[125] a notion which, especially in comparison with the ancient European tradition, nourished a kind of academic familiarity.[126] This "Renaissance Orientale"[127] developed in exactly the same intellectual climate that made Whitman's *Passage to India* and Goethe's *West-Eastern Divan*[128] possible. On the other hand, there is India's modern reality, "burden of conscience for white Christians [...] [ready to] bring them Western morality and ethics",[129] in that line of thinking–a reality that could musically only be disappointing, for in the chain of perception it followed the study of ancient treatises on music: "Proper knowledge of the Orient proceeded from a thorough study of the classical texts, and only after that to an application of those texts to the modern Orient."[130] The contemporary society was accordingly perceived by the Europeans as the demise[131] of that glorious period, and a British musicologist wrote succinctly about its music in 1914: "It is all very sad."[132]

The results of Edward Said's study *Orientalism* cannot be applied to India indiscriminately. Some of the basic mechanisms at work that Said identified for the Arabian colonial area, however, can also be traced in India:

> Faced with the obvious decreptitude and political impotence of the modern Oriental, the European Orientalist found it his duty to rescue some portion of a lost, past classical Oriental grandeur in order to "facilitate ameliorations" in the present Orient.[133]

With this background, European texts often leave the purely descriptive level to enter the functional level: the text is written to influence, trying to persuade its readers that action is necessary[134] – all from the ethical perspective. The motivations and intentions are widely diverging, and I can detect three clearly distinctive and typical patterns of argumentation that occur often in the English discourse: those that appear in the writings of A.H. Fox Strangways, Margaret Cousins and Ernest Clements. Other authors have brought forward similar or related notions: Maud McCarthy and Ananda Kentish Coomaraswamy come to mind. Here, I shall focus on the three first-mentioned authors and mention other writers in passing only.

That no texts in Hindi or Urdu are considered here narrows the view on the matter, but the fact that the discussion about the harmonium was largely conducted in English makes up for this, however. English has been an official language in India since 1835, and at the time in question it had become a scientific language already; in a discourse in which European influence is debated and in which several Europeans took part, English was the most suitable language. This does not mean that there are no texts in Hindi and Urdu; but these texts form a quantitative minority, and constructive contributions to the discussion were not seldom translated to English.[135]

Common to all, Europeans and Indians alike, there is a basic fear that with the harmonium the independent Indian culture will soon be completely Europeanised.

A.H. Fox Strangways

> If the Mohammedan star singer knew that the harmonium with which he accompanies himself was ruining his chief asset, his musical ear, and if the girl who learns the pianoforte could see that all the progress she made was a sure step towards her own detonalization as if she crossed the black water and never returned – they would pause before they laid such sacrilegious hands on Saraswati.[136]

Fox Strangways wrote this in 1914, at a time when the harmonium was a common sight in music circles. Fox Strangways" personal dismay cannot be missed, and one can almost detect a subliminal rage. I find his choice of words and images very interesting: He refers to the "Mohammedan star singer", most likely meaning *ghazal* and *qawwali* performers, but primarily "light" music. At first glance the metaphor of the singer laying hands on Saraswati when using a harmonium seems curious, for Saraswati is the goddess of knowledge and among other things of music (one of her attributes is the *vina*). Either Fox Strangways" somewhat strained attempt to use Indian idioms fails thoroughly, or he associates the use of the harmonium (for him a clearly negative connotation) with Muslim musicians. This corresponds to the indeterminate European resentment against Muslims not uncommon in his times[137] – it could, however, just as well refer to the radical Hinduistic counterpart, namely that mistrust of all the Muslim 'intruders' threatening "Mother India", and who are stereotyped as martial and unmusical.[138] The latter seems to me to be the most probable, taking Fox Strangways" other comments and writings into account. This indicates a rigid attempt to defend not the Indian, but the Hindu position as the only one with an exclusive claim to the "truth" against threats from outside, which manifests itself in the Muslims as the most recent conquerors from a historical perspective. This way a considerable part of Indian musical practice is simply rejected or branded as inferior from the outset.

The question arises as to what is behind such a notion. In my opinion, the key lies in the colonial rulers' ambivalent perception of India mentioned earlier. The humanistic "discovery" par excellence of the late 18th and early 19th centuries, namely the cultural and philological kinship between ancient Aryan and ancient Greek cultures, underwent an intensive reappraisal by Friedrich Max Müller (1823–1900) among others, and reinforced a kind of academic euphoria. The titles of many European and Europe-oriented musicological studies [*Hindu music* (Tagore), *On the Musical Modes of the Hindus* (Jones), *Music of the Hindus* (Nathan), *On the Hindu Division of the Octave* (Bosanquet) and many others, see bibliography; the writings of Willard form a notable exception[139]] suggest what much of the study of Indian music is about: to portray the original, "purely" Indian and therefore Hindu music, the product of a related high culture long gone, and with which there is a certain, freshly rediscovered kinship, India being the "mother of Aryan nations".[140] To conserve this abstracted and historicised music, far removed from reality, in archival purity is understood as an unspoken scientific duty, with differing degrees of self-reflection.

The polemic that some authors level at the harmonium itself is amazing, not only against its use in Indian music. Again it is Fox Strangways who makes no secret of his antipathy. He describes a performance situation and his brief conversation with the singer:

> The songstress wanted to accompany herself on the harmonium, until I pointed out that it would be much in her way when she pulled the string of the cradle, and that the sound of it might prevent the baby from going to sleep.[141]

Needless to say, the situation is grotesque: Fox Strangways collects songs for documentary purposes by having them sung to him, yet manipulates the singer's decision regarding the instrumentation so that the performance conforms to his notion of the pure Brahman character of Indian music. For him the harmonium is "[...] the serious menace to Indian music [...]"[142] – even though, as he remarks in the following sentence, it has already spread to the last corners of the country. Fox Strangways' wording uses metaphors – like in the following quotation – that refer to objects of comparison that appear ancient, but never to objects associated with modernity or modern life:

> It dominates the theatre, and desolates the hearth; and before long it will, if it does not already, desecrate the temple. Besides its deadening effect on a living art it

> falsifies it by being out of tune with itself. [...] A worse fault is that it is a borrowed instrument, constructed originally to minister to the less noble kind of music of other lands.[143]

Fox Strangways writes about a "living art". His perception of what he is hearing in India is preconfigured by extra-musical categories: he rejects common, basically identical musical structures between Hindus and Muslims[144] by differentiating according to religious affiliation, which is musically untenable. Assimilating, absorbing and rejecting musical developments and foreign influences – e.g. Muslim-Persian ones – are processes that constitute a living music culture. But this is not what Fox Strangways meant when he used the term "living art"; he therefore has another intention, which is primarily to contrast it with the "deadening effect" he envisions.

His second argument against the harmonium in the quotation above is that it is a foreign instrument. In this context it becomes clear what he means by a "living art": Hinduistic music without European influence. With this he apparently has in mind the music he has come across, only without the harmonium, because another "deadening effect" of this magnitude he does not see.[145] Only by dismissing past musical influences from outside (e.g. from Afghani and Persian cultures) and the selective perception that such a dismissal entails, he can hold this view.

Fox Strangways never got to know the "pure" music culture he had in mind; when he arrived in India the harmonium was firmly established, as he writes himself. Even if there were classical music without harmonium (as there is today), the mainstream had accepted the instrument – *i.e.* the music possessed the required flexibility that Fox Strangways denounces so emphatically.

Fox Strangways' notion of Indian music is not based upon the musical reality he perceived. He argues on the basis of an Orientalist ideal, which he defends for the reasons mentioned above.

The second striking point in the quotation above is connected with qualitative moral concepts. Fox Strangways writes that the instrument is not only imported – implying to the reader that this disqualifies the instrument from the outset – but that it also is "constructed originally to minister to the less noble kind of music of other lands". He operates therefore – if only in subordinate clauses – with European moral concepts, which he applies to his analysis of Indian music. Even if at first glance he seems to try to assume[146] and defend the indigenous position: his view is fundamentally Orientalist. Said writes that such a combination of reality and projected ideal is in no way uncommon in the colonial context:

> [...] the imaginative examination of things Oriental was based more or less exclusively upon a sovereign Western consciousness out of whose unchallenged centrality an Oriental world emerged, first according to general ideas about who or what was an Oriental, then according to a detailed logic governed not simply by empirical reality but by a battery of desires, repressions, investments, and projections.[147]

Margaret Cousins

Margaret Cousins' rejection is not any less passionate than that of Fox Strangways, yet hers has an entirely different background. Cousins (1878–1954) was the wife of Irish poet James Cousins. The Cousins joined the theosophical movement of Annie Besants and moved to India. Margaret Cousins is legendary for her conversation with Mohandas Gandhi, in which she convinced him of the importance of Indian women for the independence movement.

Cousins' main text on music[148] shows that she, contrary to Fox Strangways, has no sound knowledge of music, and flaws in her argumentation are remarkably often based on factual mistakes she makes when referring to European music. For her the harmonium is "the most sinister influence in Eastern music today",[149] with its inability to produce "quarter tones" it is completely unsuitable for the performance of Indian music, and its harsh sound disqualifies it for accompaniment. Her antipathy against the instrument is not only aimed at its use in Indian music, she also sees no right for the harmonium to exist in Europe:

> [...] Indians mistakenly think [the harmonium] is an honourable part of Western music. It is only the equipment of Central European beggars. [...] It is unworthy of both East and West. [...] It is no wonder it is called harmonium, for it works "harm" wherever it goes![150]

Like Fox Strangways, Cousins, projects onto Indian music her own moral concepts, which unlike Fox Strangways" are even less based on musical reasons than on her own experiences in Europe. In the same book it becomes clear that Cousins only saw the harmonium used as a beggar's instrument in Austria,[151] and never got to know any other use of the instrument. The harmonium's success in India she explains as follows:

> [...] the glamour of being a Western instrument gave it an entree into homes where indigenous music [was] forbidden because of the bad moral odour which had unfortunately attached itself to the professional musician.[152]

Cousins sees the reason for the Indians' use of the harmonium in their faulty assumption that the instrument is accepted in Europe. She implies that the instrument basically is bought for prestige reasons, but that it has the opposite effect – which Indian harmonium players, however, do not know. Cousins' musical arguments are limited to the two elements mentioned: timbre and tuning. Her criticism of the sound quality can be verified in other sources, just like the problem with equal temperament. Yet Cousins argues that the instrument has to be able to produce "quarter tones". It is obvious that she means *shrutis*, but the term "quarter tones" is factually wrong, as was known especially in India at the time (1935) because of relevant musicological texts,[153] also in English.

The Orientalist moment in Cousins' texts is much weaker than in Fox Strangways'. She projects her moral conception without a detour over a constructed ideal of Indian music. She can do this, because although she admires the ancient traditions of India, she cannot put them above the current form of musical performance as was academic fashion at the time. On a musical level, she does not compare Indian past with Indian present, but Indian present with European present – and that within her own scope of experience and ideology. In keeping with her anti-colonial ideals, the result is that Indian music has a much higher level of development than European music.[154]

Her tacitly formulated reason for this assumption is obviously based on a concept of the coherence of religion, spirituality and music – a view that is in line with her closeness to the theosophical society. She defends her concept of Indian music not in favour of a historico-cultural dimension or something similar, but as her personal religious sphere which is threatened by the association with prejudices the harmonium brought along from Europe.

Her way of arguing is not fuelled by the academic impetus that prompted Orientalists like Fox Strangways to take action against the harmonium; it is rather the esoteric aspect that, in combination with European ideological concepts, makes it her personal cause to curb the harmonium's spread in India.

Ernest Clements

Ernest Clements (born 1873) was an officer of the ICS (Indian Civil Service), the British executive administrative body. Clements sees the urgent need for the 'musical restoration' of India, because Indian music is suffering from two destructive forces: on the one hand the general confusion regarding the traditional music theory, on the other hand the system's demise caused by contact with Western music:

> Contact with the West has resulted in a blend of Indian music with European intonation, a combination in the highest degree inartistic and likely to prove more harmful than the neglect of centuries.[155]

Clements' observations are sober and analytical compared to those of Fox Strangways and Cousins. He writes about the harmonium: "Those teachers who promote the sale of tempered harmoniums, and make use of them in the classroom, are proving their own incapacity to guide the musical renaissance of their country."[156] He is talking not of "high art", but of general musical training. In spite of the negative formulation he quasi-suggests a concrete possibility to improve the situation, namely to avoid the use of the harmonium in musical training. Clements' rejection of the instrument becomes not less embracing through that, and the fact that he sees a need for action here does not limit it to music training. His criticism of the instrument is based on the instrument's tempered tuning.

Clements' approach differs from preceding and contemporary positions because it is constructive: with the so-called *shruti*-harmonium he designs an instrument that is able to play 22 pitches per octave. Retrospectively it is difficult to establish who participated in which way in the "invention". What can be verified is that the fixation of the "Indian scale" – which never gained universal acceptance – can be traced back to two persons: the Indian musicologist K.B. Deval (1847–1931), who made calculations on the monochord, and the singer Abdul Karim Khan, with whose help Deval tried to verify his results. These results were put into relation with ancient music theory, and were implemented in the *shruti*-harmonium.

The instrument was designed[157] by Teofil Kot(y)kiewicz, the successor of Peter Titzen[158] (Vienna), and patented at a later stage by the company Moore & Moore (London).[159] At the All-India Music Conference of 1916, initiated by Bhatkande to "preserve"[160] Indian music, it was presented and discussed; it found favour neither before nor after this event. "It was built five years ago and I am informed on the best authorities that there has been no enquiry whatsoever for it, much less demand"[161], S. J. Sarkes wrote in 1915.

In the *shruti*-harmonium Clements sees the solution for the dilemma:

> [...] there is hardly any form of soft scale which cannot be obtained from its keyboard. Our position is, that if any ordinary Indian scale be found which cannot be produced on the Indian harmonium, that scale must either be "capricious" or to quote from Mr. Ellis' 'tempered'. We believe that in the realm of the art of homophonic music [...] capricious, arbitrary or artificial scales do not exist. We know that individual singers habitually sing wrong notes [...] This however is not art.[162]

Clements regarded his tuning as universal.[163] But his method is not correct: a theory that claims to be universal yet dismisses other existing tunings as "capricious" becomes absurd. Thus also Clements does not want to preserve the reality, but undo the damage that has been done by European influence – and again the objective is an ideal that has no real content, and above all is an ideal on which no consensus has been reached. The uncertainty as to how the octave is divided stems from the fact that there is no constant scale – the Indian scale varies from *raga* to *raga* and, as will be discussed in the second part of this book, from singer to singer. Apart from that, there is general disagreement on the "fundamental" scale offering orientation. The *raga*-dependent variation of single pitches presupposes flexibility regarding intonation – a flexibility that renders any prescriptive tuning system like Clements' impossible. Why the harmonium's "wrong" intonation is preferred to the more accurate tuning of other instruments will be investigated further below. Without doubt the difficulties presented by a manual with 22 keys per octave added to the *shruti*-harmonium's difficulty in gaining a foothold – similar to the Janko-manual in Europe.

Clements' harmonium was designed in Vienna and patented in London – a peculiar combination for an instrument that was to be used in India. Clements was not the only one trying to construct instruments able to deal with the Indian division of the octave. Govindrao Tembe built such an instrument, which he played personally and which he probably adapted to his own practical needs. It has 48 keys per octave and although it still exists, it is not played any more. The reason put forward for this is that the special tuning is "very difficult".[164] Apparently the exact tuning is not known, the division of the octave into 48 steps does not seem to correlate with any common Indian music theory. In my knowledge all other attempts at constructing harmoniums with an extended number of pitches were made by Europeans.

R.H.M. Bosanquet, a London professor for piano, had, in collaboration with Hermann von Helmholtz, a harmonium built with 24–84 steps per octave by the London harmonium maker T.A. Jennings;[165] the Berlin instrument maker Johannes W. Kewitsch built a so-called "enharmonic harmonium" with 20 keys per octave, based on a design by Shohe Tanaka;[166] the Leipzig professor of physics Arthur von Oettingen designed an "orthotonophonium", a harmonium with 53 steps per octave, patented in 1914 and built by Schiedmayer (Stuttgart);[167] in Glasgow, Colin Brown built a similar instrument, which he called a "Voice Harmonium".[168] [169]

The motivation for building these instruments did not stem from musical practice; they were rather experiments in acoustics that convinced those who had the instruments built (Helmholtz, among others) that equal temperament was a makeshift solution and that pure tuning was desirable as a fundamental principle in European music.[170]

This position arose after the analysis of non-European scales, but the "target culture" originally was Europe. The reason the harmonium was used for experiments was not because it had any special qualities; it was the free reeds' ability to maintain their tuning that made it the instrument of choice for experiments in pure tuning.[171] The prime goal was to have an instrument to demonstrate the tuning with. Only afterwards it was discovered that the Indian subcontinent was a potential market for this kind of instrument; an article on the Indian scale, published by Bosanquet in 1877,[172] in which he virtually propagates "his" manual design for use in Indian music, is in my knowledge the first transfer of European efforts to the Indian system.

Indian demands for such an instrument at an earlier stage are not known to me; naturally there are Indians opposed to the harmonium, but the need for an innovation of this kind is never expressed. It seems, therefore, that the impulse for building *shruti*-harmoniums mainly came from European side, without an acute practical need having been formulated. This assumption is confirmed by the fact that musicians never accepted the instrument.[173]

What motivated Europeans to modify an established instrument "for the Indians" so strongly that it was possible to play microtonal intervals on it? Again it seems to be the notion of a cultural kinship, reinforced by the idea of a "universal scale".

Bhavanrav A. Pingle's writings stand out from the remaining comments on the harmonium. Writing in the 1890s, he recommends the instruments for early musical training "to cultivate a taste in youths".[174] He does acknowledge the instrument's shortcomings, such as its incapacity to produce *mind*,[175] but the only real shortcoming he sees in the instrument (which he also refers to as "new accompaniment"[176]) is 'that when it gets out of order or tune it cannot soon be attuned except by a professional repairer".[177]

Almost all other contributions concerning the harmonium are negative towards the instrument. No written conflict ensued, probably because the contributions were mostly taken note of by other theoreticians who had a similar hostile attitude towards the harmonium. Musicological texts were written and taken note of by musicologists, and hardly ever by musicians.

The small [?? compared to what was written about other instruments at the time this is a lot] number of English texts by local authors expressing themselves negatively about the harmonium is surprising. The rigour of Rabindranath Tagore's *bon mot* "bane of Indian music",[178] quoted so often and also here, is strongly moderated by his letter of 1888 to the harmonium company Dwarkin & Co., in which he writes after having played the early Indian harmonium model: "There is no doubt that this instrument is particularly useful for Indian music" (see figure 12).[179] The crux of this change of attitude is that this positive judgement is almost thirty years older than the cited statement from his *Reminiscences,* and also precedes the ban of the harmonium in Shantiniketan (and the Marris College of Music in Lucknow, later named as Bhathkande College of Music, in 1930)[180]; if it had been the other way around and Tagore's opinion had changed to a more positive one, one could have assumed that there had been improvements in tone quality and developments that caused such a change of opinion. Yet this is not the case, and Tagore's approval of the instrument is strongly limited by the later document. It is possible that the phrase "bane of Indian music" was strained the few times it was quoted.[181] What is obvious, however, is that Tagore was by no means always clearly against the harmonium.

K.D. Banerjee, an author who seems to have an ambiguous stance toward the instrument, in 1886 calls the harmonium an "imperfect importation from Europe" doing "great injury to the human voice".[182] His main criticism is the usage of the harmonium in early music training "to mask the voice"[183] and its incapacity to render fine melodic and rhythmic nuances, which he believes has a "deadening and destructive effect on Indian music".[184] Only little later in the same text, however, Banerjee lauds the instrument's timbre.[185] Banerjee's translator's comments are sometimes difficult to distinguish from his translation of Banerjee's original text, which at times makes it unclear whether he is translating Banerjee or putting forward his own, clearly negative opinion. Unlike Banerjee himself, who sees advantages in the harmonium, commentator Banerji is strictly against the instrument; he even uses the same words to express his indignation as Fox Strangways, which suggests that he has been influenced by Strangways' writings. And indeed, for further arguments, he refers to Fox Strangways and Ernest Clements.[186]

Further, there is Babu Nanak Prasad, who in his *Indian Music. Scientific and Practical,* published in 1906, considers the usage of the harmonium to be a symptom of a general and continuous musical decline in India.[187] However, the general negative undertone that characterizes Fox Strangways" and Banerjee's writings, among others, is missing. Interestingly, the "... greatest injury to our music"..., in Prasad's appraisal, is not done by the harmonium, but by the *esraj.*[188]

None of those criticising the use of the instrument assumes an objective, distanced position: factors of a personal nature and on a higher level constantly influence perception and how opinions are formed, and the "duty" to "help" India undergo an overdue development with the aid of the more advanced European music and acoustic analysis often assumes an almost missionary character. This does not come from nowhere:

> Western musicologists and Indians alike like Tagore, Mudaliyar, Deval, Pingle, Bhatkande, and others were discussing music at a time when the power struggle between colonizer and colonized was about to reach its peak, and music as a cultural form was caught up in this, if merely as a side-show to the main action.[189]

Whether the starting position is of academic, esoteric or any other nature: "The modern Orientalist was, in his view, a hero rescuing the Orient from the obscurity, alienation, and strangeness which he himself had properly distinguished."[190]

Fig. 12: Advertising material of Dwarkin & Son, Kolkata, quoting Rabindranath Tagore's 1888 letter to the company.

II.3.2 After 1940

The year 1940 marks a crossroads for the harmonium, because for the first time an institution reacted to the harmonium's bad reputation: the British-controlled state radio station, All India Radio[191] banned the instrument from the air. This meant that musicians whose performance was broadcast were not allowed to use the instrument, also not for rehearsal or practising purposes. It also was not allowed to be used in theatre or radio plays, not even for acoustic "effects"[192] – the rejection of the instrument was so pervasive that even in the extra-musical context of sound effects its sound was perceived as something very negative. Considering the banishment of *baijis* and *tawaifs* from A.I.R. broadcasts six years later (in 1946),[193] it becomes evident that the ban of the harmonium was part of the station's then-current policy, and it gives an interesting twist to it.

The ban commenced on March 1, 1940;[194] a directive went out to all local radio stations that all harmoniums owned by the stations were to be sold. At the time A.I.R. employed a significant number of musicians, and because it also offered permanent jobs for musicians (their salaries graded according to the musicians' "class") it had an imaginably strong influence on their social position, and this power was also used.[195] A.I.R.'s economical and social influence was exceeded by no other institution or person, and accordingly the scope of its directives reached into the musicians' sphere of musical and artistic decisions. For this reason, A.I.R. had the potential to counter "problematic trends" in Indian music, as can be concluded from a report by the Briton Lionel Fielden, a founding member of A.I.R. The aims of the radio station were:[196] " (1) to see to it that *ragas* were interpreted according to the rules; "a departure from tradition should not be permitted", " (2) to promote an (artificial) hybridisation of light and classical Indian music, catering to the tastes of a broad audience yet without diluting Indian music, and " (3) aiming at a definite breaking away from present standards" by the "adoption of notation and harmony". This sound like the familiar pattern in the public discussion, and the directives seem to have originated only from European members of the All India Radio management.

The harmonium's ban from the programme of the radio-monopolist seems to stem directly from the British director of the 'Western Music' department at the central radio station in Delhi, John Foulds.[197] Interestingly enough, Foulds was very involved in the area of so-called "fusion"; as director of the "AIR Orchestra" he often experimented with Indian music and harmony.[198] He seems to have distinguished clearly between "fusion" and "pure" Indian classical music: otherwise his initiative against the harmonium – which ultimately strived for a "pure" Indian music – cannot be understood. In *The Indian Listener* (A.I.R.'s magazine) of March 1 1940, Foulds wrote an article with the heading "Harm-omnium", in which he calls the instrument un-Indian and unmusical. On March 22, A.I.R. broadcast a programme casting light on the decision to ban the instrument: *Herr Monium – Rise and Fall of a Dictator.*[199] Even if 1940 is early for such a clear allusion: the German form of address "Herr" seems to be meant as an allusion to the Nazi regime and the Second World War, particularly because of the obvious similarity to the title of Brecht's opera *Rise and Fall of the City of Mahagonny.*

The ban prompted different reactions. Naturally, neither the musicians for whom the harmonium was a fixed element of an ensemble nor the harmonium makers were exactly thrilled. But faced with the economical power that A.I.R. yielded, these people had no choice but to adapt to the new situation. There were also positive reactions – among others, Rabindranath Tagore is said to have nodded approval in a letter.[200]

It was All India Radio's objective not only to broadcast a "harmonium-free" programme conforming to its own standards, but also to have a lasting effect on the music culture of all of India. Such an endeavour was ambitious for the time, given the fact that the harmonium had long established itself as standard instrument. It comes surprisingly late, which is surely in part due to the fact that All India Radio only existed since 1936 and that radio broadcasting only came to India in 1924. In the early tumultuous years other culturo-political and also technical matters seemed to be of higher priority[201] – yet apart from that, also 1924 (or 1936) would have been a late point for such an attempt.

What effect did the ban have retrospectively? First of all, it caused all harmonium players to be discharged.[202] But musicians permanently employed by A.I.R. invariably performed outside their regular jobs, i.e. their musical activity was not entirely limited to the radio stations. In this "free"' domain the A.I.R. regulations, of course, had no effect, and if singers preferred to be accompanied by harmoniums rather than *sarangis* in their non-A.I.R. work it had no consequence for them. Those responsible hoped that the ban of the harmonium would usher in a revival of the *sarangi*-tradition. But this never happened, which shows how much more influence concert life had on the Indian music scene than radio or television – and perhaps how far-reaching the *sarangi's* traditional social connotations were.

The wide use of the harmonium seemed to be unimpressed by the A.I.R. ban, and no negative effects can be diagnosed.

The A.I.R. ban

Time and again petitions were handed to A.I.R., requesting a lift of the ban.[203] In 1970, A.I.R. presented a symposium on the harmonium, where the future A.I.R. position regarding the instrument was to be discussed and where prominent members of the Indian music scene were to present their standpoints. The official symposium report shows that it was much less about the harmonium than about finding an acceptable course of action for the future.

> For over three decades the Harmonium has suffered a total ban [on A.I.R.]. [...] The Harmonium has proved an ubiquitous instrument. Despite its lowly status it has been persistently present on the concert stage, in the class-room and in theatre and film-music. This has led A.I.R. to seriously review the question of its use in broadcasts of classical and light music.[204]

Seven lectures were presented at the symposium, and each lecture sparked a heated discussion. Some speakers were for and some against the harmonium's acceptance, and the paradigm change in the speakers' argumentation has a real background: India was independent now, and the actively participating members of the symposium were all Indians.

In his lecture, P.V. Subramaniam basically formulates the result of the entire symposium:

> It [i.e. the harmonium] has established itself as a popular instrument; it has helped the initiation of laymen into the tonal mysteries and outlines of classical music and has been a faithful aid for ailing voices. All I ask is that it be reckoned as one of the many varieties of our musical instruments and not treated as an outcast. I plead for an immediate ban on this form of untouchability.[205]

This view was opposed diametrically by S.N. Ratanjankar: "Does the instrument after all deserve such attention to drive us to hold a seminar on it at a cost equal, almost, to the cost of a dozen or more harmoniums? I ask myself."[206] The discussion in the seminar shows that the harmonium obviously did deserve it – irrespective of the seminar actually having no other purpose than to approve of a decision which had been made long before in practice.

All the speakers were willing to allow the harmonium, even if only within a certain scope. The width of this scope depended on two viewpoints: (1) Is the use of the instrument limited to light and semi-classical music? (2) Does it make sense to allow its use only as a solo instrument, but not as an accompanying instrument, or vice versa? How profound the process of change was still active even at this time can be seen in the fact that the same argument is used for opposite aims. This is the case with the argument that the harmonium helps a singer to conceal minor vocal flaws: P.V. Subramaniam uses it when arguing for the harmonium; the traditional standpoint disapproves of such use.[207] The most common arguments for the harmonium as accompanying instrument are the following:

1. Not only average, but also singers regarded as outstanding (Bade Ghulam Ali Khan, Abdul Karim Khan and others) used the instrument.
2. There is no sufficient number of *sarangi*-players any more to meet the demand for accompanists.
3. The timbre of the free reeds suits (a) sonorous male voices well, is (b) through the combination of different stops more able to accommodate different voices than any other instrument (cf. the argumentation regarding high male voices).
4. The harmonium does not need to be tuned, is easily transportable and can produce – contrary to the *sarangi* – a reliable flow of sound.
5. The harmonium has become an irreplaceable tool in basic music education.

Those opposing the harmonium – clearly the minority – argued against the harmonium with the following arguments:

1. The harmonium is unable to play *shrutis*. That means that certain *ragas* cannot be played properly,
2. which is exacerbated by the fact that certain ornaments cannot be produced on the instrument.
3. The instrument's success is based on the fact that it's so easy to learn to play it. This argumentation, which received no closer scrutiny during the symposium, is indirectly based on the often inaccurate but common notion that traditionally trained musicians have a poor general education. A ban of the harmonium, in this line of argument, would force musicians to occupy themselves more intensively with the intricacies of Indian music and thus lead to a more solid musical basis.

Point (1) was countered by the harmonium's advocates with the argument that technology to produce *shrutis* on the harmonium already exists and that such instruments can be built without delay. With regard to the ornaments, it was noted that a good player can come very close to the ideal. The argument that the harmonium is a "foreign" instrument is mentioned, but plays only a marginal role.

After the symposium, A.I.R. made the following decisions concerning the ban:

> In the wake of the Seminar, and with due consideration to the findings and views of the experts, A.I.R. has issued a directive partially removing the ban on the Harmonium in the following types of programmes;
>
> *(i)* Top grade and A grade artists may use the Harmonium as an accompanying instrument in classical, light classical and light vocal music.

> *(ii)* Approved Quawaali parties of all grades who utilise the Harmonium in public performances may also use it in broadcasts.
> *(iii)* Approved choral groups of all grades who utilise the Harmonium in public performances may also use it in broadcasts.
> *(iv)* Specially produced items in classical, light classical and light programmes may use the Harmonium on the advice of the Producer concerned.
>
> The ban on the Harmonium will remain in programmes of lower grade artists. No solo performances of the Harmonium will be broadcast.[208]

The situation preceding this decision seems paradoxical – the country's biggest disseminator of music initiates a discussion of a question to which musical practice has found an answer long ago. This is based on a concept of tradition which had been at least a matter of discussion for decades, but which also appears in a strongly idealised form; the divergence of tradition and ideal and reality is addressed tacitly. It is the musicians who constantly re-invent the tradition, and not ancient treatises which had a descriptive rather than normative character at the time they were written. Even the prominent role of the radio could not prevent outstanding musicians from using the harmonium, and it also failed to convey a negative value judgement. At the end of the day, it was this insight that raised the ban.

* * *

"It is really surprising that no Indian artist or musicologist had initiated the ban of harmonium",[209] Goswami wrote in 1996. The ban was mainly initiated by Britons, but this fact is anything but surprising regarding the course of the preceding public discourse. The ban's implementation follows the same European and Orientalist concepts as the general rejection of the instrument – even in 1940.

As far as both – ban and public discussion – are concerned, there were always opponents and advocates of the instrument on the Indian and European side. The question as to who expresses himself in which way is first of all not a matter of contents but of the medium used. Decisive is not whether the English language is used, but in general whether written language is used. With reference to the 1970 A.I.R. symposium, Deshpande remarked:

> Ours is indeed a musically backward country where academians tend to remain cut off from the practising performers and the performers, who only sing and please cannot or do not think or speak. They simply avoid the company of academicians![210]

This implied communication problem between musicians and musicologists exists to a lesser degree to this day – a phenomenon not unique to the Indian subcontinent. Yet it has nothing to do with being 'backward', as Deshpande reckons, but is a consequence of the oral tradition. 'Great musicians' were not expected to be able to read and write, also not in the 20th century; knowledge of a great number of compositions and pure musical expertise were key qualifications to be a good musician. Musicians did not need to be able to express themselves analytically with regards to music or to reflect their own creations rationally.

Because of this distance between musicians and theoreticians, Indian writing and reflection on music has a very theoretical perspective. Perhaps nowhere is this clearer than in the case of the harmonium: to this day there are theoreticians and a few musicians who claim that the harmonium is unsuitable for Indian music, but the reality of the musicians looks entirely different. There is a connection between everyday music practice and music theory, but the one does not always presuppose the other entirely.

Historically, these theoretical views are expressed by an academically educated Indian "elite", whereas academic education at the time is inseparably associated with a strong British influence for institutional reasons alone. Active musicians and especially harmonium players do not necessarily belong to this "class" which has the ability to take advantage of its intellectual capacities in the colonial context. "The subaltern cannot speak", says Spivak's post-colonial theorem;[211] harmonium players can be seen as "subalterns" in this sense. They can express themselves and do so, but in entirely different channels than those of the dominant discussion. The texts I have dealt with in this chapter are colonialism's narration of Indian culture, disarticulating the tradition, independently from whether they were written by Indians or Europeans – only those able to navigate colonial communicational structures can take part in this form of discourse.

Thus it can be explained why also Indians active in the field of musicology and participating in the discussion refer to ancient treatises before the current musical reality is taken into consideration: the cleft between musician and musicologist entails a different form of expression, and this has decisive effects on the literature concerning music in general and ever further reaching consequences on the sources available today.

In colonial times, Indian musicology was influenced directly by European colonialism – which caused certain patterns of thought and frames of reference to be adopted:

> British intrusion in the eighteenth century [...] so disrupted the social system of the traditional elite of Bengal that when Orientalists did provide a golden age-dark age polarity many Bengalis readily accepted it.[212]

If it seems as if the prevalent attitude towards the harmonium was one of explicit rejection, this certainly is representative for the texts available. However, it is not representative for the entire spectrum of opinions at the time – the musical reality speaks a different language. On the contrary, written texts represent only a small extract from the big picture, in which oral and musical discourses lie more submerged. While academic observers, music aficionados and Orientalists were busy ranting, musicians made the decision to incorporate the harmonium into their musical world. The reasons for this will crystallise out in the following chapters.

Endnotes

1. Peter Manuel [*The Harmonium in Indian and Indo-Caribbean Music. From Colonial Tool to Nationalist Icon*, in: *Free-Reed Journal* vol. 1 (1999)] presumes that the harmonium was introduced to India in the late 18th century.
2. H.D. Banerjea, *A Comprehensive Self-Instructor for the Setar, Esrar, Violin, Flute, and Harmonium*, Calcutta 1868; mentioned in C.R. Day, *The Music and Musical Instruments of Southern India and the Deccan*, London 1891, p. 160. Joep Bor kindly pointed me to this source. Krishna Dhan Banerjee's *Harmonium Shiksha* dates from 1899. Kasliwal ascribes it to Nandlal; see Suneera Kasliwal, *Classical Musical Instruments*, New Delhi 2001, p. 257, who states 1885 as the year in which the harmonium was mentioned for the first time. She is alluding to Krishna Dhan Banerjee's *Gita Sutra Sar*, written in Bengali and available in the translation of Himansu Sekhar Banerji (*Translator's Explantions and Notes to Krishna Dhan Banerjee's Gita Sutra Sar, vol. 2, part 2*, Calcutta 1941). The *Harmonium Sútra* was written, also in Bengali, by Sourindro Mohan Tagore in 1874.
3. A prominent example of such an instrument is the *sheng*, of which Marin Mersenne included an illustration in his *Harmonie Universelle*. See e.g. Christian Ahrens, *Zur Entwicklung des Harmoniums und seiner Terminologie*, in: Christian Ahrens & Gregor Klinke (ed.), *Das Harmonium in Deutschland. Bau, wirtschaftliche Bedeutung und musikalische Nutzung eines 'historischen' Musikinstrumentes*, Frankfurt a. M. 1996, p. 22.
4. Ian Woodfield, *The Keyboard Recital in Oriental Diplomacy*, in: *Journal of the Royal Musical Association*, 115 (1990), pp. 33–62, here p. 47 et seq.

5. Ian Woodfield, *Music of the Raj. A Social and Economic History of Music in Late Eighteenth-Century Anglo-Indian Society*, Oxford 2000, passim.
6. Ibid., p. 4.
7. Arthur W.J.G. Ord-Hume, in a letter to me dated August 26, 2003 (unpublished), p. 1 et seq.
8. Napier's 1994 (see note 1) study is an exception.
9. As Peter Manual does [*Harmonium* (see note 3)]. He assumes the "late eighteenth century" as a time frame – in any case at a point in time when even experiments with free reeds in Europe were just starting and a useful, harmonium-like instrument cannot be imagined.
10. See Woodfield, *Music of the Raj* (see note 7), p. 15 et seq., especially the table providing an overview of the ships' cargoes that imported musical instruments among other things. The other three large British settlements of Surat, Mumbai and Madras offer similar import statistics.
11. Loke Nath Ghose, *The Modern history of the Indian Chiefs, Rajas, Zamindars, &c.: Part II The Native Aristocracy and Gentry*, Calcutta 1881, p. 173.
12. Banerjee, *Gita Sutra Sar* (see note 4), p. 31.
13. Amal Das Sharma, *Musicians of India, Past and Present. Gharanas of Hindustani Music and Genealogies*, Calcutta 1993, p. 108.
14. Ibid.
15. This information comes from Pratap Ghosh, director of the harmonium-building firm Dwarkin & Son Ltd., Kolkata (conversation on 16 May 2003), as well as the company's flyer titled *Dwarkin made it first in the world – Dwarkin does it best in the world,* printed 1997.
16. For further details about music history and culture within this sphere see e.g. Sumanta Banerjee, *The Parlour and the Streets. Elite and Popular Culture in Nineteenth Century Calcutta*, Calcutta 1998, especially chapter 4 about Elite Culture in Nineteenth Century Calcutta, pp. 147–198.
17. In many sources, Jotindro Tagore (1849-1925) is credited with not only having the harmonium established within the *Brahmo Samaj*, but also with having it introduced to India (see the reference given in note 35). See, for instance, Sourindo Mohun Tagore's *Universal History of Music, Compiled from diverse sources, together with various original notes on Hindu music*, Calcutta 1896, e.g. p. 84; and, for a more contemporary appraisal, Vinayak Purohit, *Arts of Transitional India - Twentieth Century*, Mumbai 1986, p. 862.
18. Ibid., p. 148.
19. The exposure to European musical culture was limited to private life; the many 'music clubs' and the like attended by the British upper class were exclusive and did not admit Indians. When Dwarakanath Tagore

became a member of a British theatre association in 1813, it caused a stir and some irritation (see a.o. Chhaya Chatterjee, *Sastriya Sangita and Music Culture through the Ages*, vol. 1, Delhi, 1996, p. 202). Knowledge of European art music remained superficial at first.

20. See Avril Ann Powell, *Muslims and Missionaries in Pre-Mutiny India*, Richmond 1993, p. 50 et seq.
21. Until the 19th century, Europeans rarely occupied themselves practically with Indian music [see Woodfield, *Music of the Raj* (see note 7)].
22. The term 'Bengali Renaissance' comprises many levels, including political processes and processes of social reform as well as cultural and religious/ philosophical dimensions.
23. The Tagore family were prominent *Samaj* members for generations. Rabindranath Tagore's novel *Gora* (Calcutta 1951) gives a contemporary impression of the character and problems of the *Bramo Samaj* society. See Napier, *Sangat* (see note 2), p. 6 et seq. for Bengal and Maharashtra in connection with the harmonium.
24. See Charles Capwell, *Marginality and Musicology in Nineteenth-Century Calcutta: The Case of Sourindro Tagore*, in: Bruno Nettl & Philip V. Bohlman (ed.), *Comparative Musicology and Anthropology of Music: Essays on the History of Ethnomusicology*, Chicago 1991, pp. 228–243, here p. 231.
25. K.N. Panikkar, *Culture, Ideology, Hegemony. Intellectuals and Social Consciousness in Colonial India*, London (3) 2001, p. 86.
26. Sourindro Mohan Tagore, cited by Capwell, *Marginality* (see note 26), p. 234.
27. Ibid., p. 233.
28. Panikkar, *Social Consciousness* (see note 27), p. 101.
29. Martin Stokes, *Introduction*, in: Martin Stokes (ed.), *Ethnicity, Identity and Music. The Musical Construction of Place*, New York 1997, pp. 1–27, here p. 5.
30. M.A. Laird, *Missionaries and Education in Bengal 1793–1837*, Oxford 1972, p. 57. The fact that the Gospel of St. Matthew was translated to Persian in 1805 at the Fort William College [Powell, *Muslims & Missionaries*, (see note 22), p. 82] indicates that the College was not intended as a foreign body within Indian society, but suggests that it was seen as an institution with a Christian mission. Independently of this, the basic canon provided tuition in the various local languages, to better prepare employees for their everyday business activities. See Capwell, *Marginality* (see note 26), p. 231 et seq.
31. Capwell, *Marginality* (see note 26), p. 233.
32. Ibid.

33. P. Banerjea, *History of Hindu Music, in:* The Bengal Magazine, *July 1880, pp. 443-455* (see note 4??), p. 452. I wish to thank Joep Bor for pointing me to this valuable source.
34. Sourindro Mohan Tagore, *Universal History* (see note 19), p. 84. Also see Napier, *Harmonium* (see note 1), p. 110 et seq.
35. Tagore, *Universal History* (see note 19), p. 84.
36. See R.K. Yajnik, *The Indian Theatre. Its Origins And its Later Developments Under European Influence*, London n.d. [1933], p. 119 et seq.
37. E.g. Othello in the Marathi-translation. See Vasant Shantaram Desai, *Years of Glory. 1880–1920*, in: *The Marathi Theatre*, Bombay 1963, p. 17. Especially Shakespeare's theatre seems to be an adequate object of comparison; sophisticated theatre for the general population, made for the masses but not only entertaining.
38. Yajnik, *The Indian Theatre* (see note 38), p. 119 et seq.
39. See Desai, *Years of Glory* (see note 39), p. 13.
40. Ibid., p. 24.
41. Ashok D. Ranade, *Stage Music of Maharashtra*, Delhi 1986, p. 58. Ranade offers no further details.
42. Ibid., p. 26. Cf. Napier, *Harmonium* (see note 1), p. 110 et seq.
43. The terminology used in the Indian literature is inconsistent, but this does not mean that different instruments were employed. Even so, the use of American reed organs and similar instruments can be verified.
44. Dyaneshwar Nadkarni, *Balgandharva and the Marathi Theatre*, Bombay 1988, p. 30.
45. Ranade, *Stage Music* (see note 43), p. 61 et seq.
46. Nadkarni, *Balgandharva* (see note 46), p. 30 et seq.
47. Sharma, *Musicians of India* (see note 15), p. 109.
48. E.g. by Vamanrao H. Deshpande, *Between two Tanpuras*, Bombay 1989, p. 29; Smt. Mutatkar, contribution to the discussion at the All India Radio-Conference on the harmonium [cited in: *Journal of the Sangeet Natak Akademi* 20 (1971), p. 25]; Premlata Sharma, *Harmonium & Hindustani Light Classical Music*, in: *Journal of the Sangeet Natak Akademi* 20 (1971), pp. 25–29, here p. 26. See also Napier, *Harmonium* (see note 1), p. 113 et seq.
49. Desai, *Years of Glory* (see note 39), p. 33.
50. Deshpande, *Between two Tanpuras* (see note 50), p. 32.
51. See Nadkarni, *Balgandharva* (see note 46), p. 21.
52. Peter Manuel, *Thumri in Historical and Stylistic Perspectives*, Delhi 1989, p. 75; also see Joep Bor, *The Voice of the Sarangi: An illustrated history of bowing in India*, in: *National Centre for the Performing Arts Quarterly Journal* 15 (3, 4) and 16 (1), pp. 1-183, p. 111.

53. Ibid., p. 75; 182.
54. On Singh, see Harendra Kishore Roy Chowdhury, *The Musicians of India (Illustrated), Part I*, Calcutta 1929, p. 4-5, and Sharma, *Musicians of India* (see note 15), p. 207.
55. Ibid., p. 207.
56. Ibid., p. 116.
57. Ibid., p. 138.
58. See Chaitanya Desai, *Thumri During the Ages*, in: *Journal of the Indian Musicological Society* 19/1, 2 (June/December 1988), *Special Book on Thumri: Traditions and Trends*, pp. 7–16, here p. 14.
59. Joep Bor cites Dilip Chandra Vedi, who said about Ganpat Rao "In that [i.e. in the use of the harmonium] he was a pioneer". Bor, *Sarangi* (see note 54), p. 111.
60. Manuel, *Thumri* (see note 54), p. 75; Napier, *Sangat* (see note 2), p. 129, p. 136.
61. Ranade, *Stage Music* (see note 43), p. 15.
62. Sharma, *Musicians of India* (see note 15); Napier, *Sangat* (see note 2), p. 137.
63. Also see Chowdhury's comment on Jamiruddin Khan in his *The Musicians of India* (see note 56), p. 59.
64. *Thumri* was not only constitutively influenced by courtesans [Manuel, *Thumri* (see note 54), p. 46] but also "female-oriented"; the usually amorous lyrics were also almost invariably written from a female perspective.
65. Manuel, *Thumri* (see note 54), p. 72 et seq.
66. Ibid., p. 73.
67. Bonnie C. Wade, *Khyal. Creativity within North India's Classical Music Tradition*, Cambridge 1984, p. 197.
68. Manuel, *Thumri* (see note 54), p. 72.
69. Conversations with Patanjali Maduskar (Mumbai, 8 April 2003), Hemang Mehta (Mumbai, 8 April 2003), Vikas Kashalkar (Pune, 4 April 2003).
70. This relates to the origins of the European free reeds, *i.e.* to Christian Gottlieb Kratzenstein's experiments and objectives. Kratzenstein wanted to build a machine able to imitate the human voice, especially its 5 vowels. [see Christian Ahrens, *Zur Frühgeschichte der Instrumente mit Durchschlagzungen in Europa*, in: Monika Lustig (Ed.), *Harmonium und Handharmonika*, Blankenburg 2002, p. 31–50, here p. 40; also Christian Ahrens, *Das Harmonium in Deutschland*, Frankfurt am Main, [2]2001, p. 22]. If the free reeds are perceived to be very similar to the human voice, it corresponds with Kratzenstein's intention.

71. Banerjee, *Gita Sutra Sar* (see note 4), p. 31.
72. Ibid., p. 116.
73. See Bor, *Sarangi* (see note 54); Bor, personal communication March 1, 2009; also see Napier, *Sangat* (see note 2), p. 125 et seq.
74. Napier, *Sangat* (see note 2), p. 123; the argumentation can be found on pp. 90–117.
75. Daniel M. Neuman, *The Life of Music in North India. The Organization of an Artistic Tradition*, Detroit 1980.
76. Wade, *Khyal* (see note 69).
77. Bor, *Sarangi* (see note 54); personal communication February 2009.
78. Bor, *Sarangi* (see note 54); also see Napier, *Sangat* (see note 2).
79. Tuning the tanpura is commonly regarded as an art. It is reserved for the singer, because only he is supposed to have to required musicality.
80. Banerjee, *Parlour and the Streets* (see note 18).
81. Because of their historical development and influences, the "classical" as well as the "folk" music traditions in India are very broad generic terms, subsuming strongly varying local and school versions. Within the context of Bengal what is mostly meant here are certain local music traditions or, for the classical tradition, certain *gharanas*.
82. It is no coincidence that the first two regions in which the harmonium established itself, Bengal and Maharashtra, were under British influence early on.
83. See e.g. M.N. Srinivas, *Social Change in Modern India*, Berkeley ^{5}1973 [^{1}1966], p. 57.
84. Ibid.
85. Sumanta Banerjee [*Parlour and the Streets* (see note 18), p. 149], mentions that within this 'Renaissance' of indigenous art forms a painting style was revived which was "imbibed from the model set by the British Royal Academy of Arts during the Victorian era".
86. Conversation 14 June 2003, Saltaire (UK). According to the visitor's guide of the Reed Organ and Harmonium Museum in Saltaire the instrument was built for Ramchunder; the possibility of the instrument being copied/adapted was expressed during the conversation.
87. Information from Pratap Ghosh, conversation in Kolkata on 16 May 2003.
88. Rekha Surya, conversation in Delhi on 29 April 2003.
89. Patanjali Maduskar, conversation in Mumbai on 7 April 2003.
90. Sharma, *Musicians of India* (see note 15), p. 247.
91. Interestingly, Jnan Ghosh [*Harmonium as a solo instrument*, in: *Sangeet Natak* 20 (1971, p. 22)], associates the alteration with Dwarkanath Tagore.

92. *Dwarkin made it first in the world* (see note 17). Cf. Napier, *Harmonium* (see note 1), p. 92 et seq.
93. Pratap Ghosh pointed out to me that the instrument's mention is a printing error; he also did not know who the original author of the text was. The term Harmoniflûte was unknown to him. Conversation in Kolkata on 16 May 2003.
94. Maria Dunkel, *Harmonikainstrumente*, in: Ludwig Finscher (ed.), *Musik in Geschichte und Gegenwart* 2, Sachteil Vol. 4, Kassel et al. 1996, col. 185. The harmoniflûte was built by manufacturers in Paris: Alexandre, Busson, Kasriel, Limonaire Frères and Mayermarix (= Mayer-Marix).
95. Michel Dieterlen, *L'Harmonium*, Villeneuve d'Asq 1999, p. 433.
96. Ibid.
97. Fr. Ducuing (ed.), *Exposition Universelle de 1867 illustrée. Publication internationale autorisée par la commission impériale*, Paris 1867, p. 269, cited in Dieterlen, *L'Harmonium* (see note 97), p. 475.
98. Oscar Comettant, *La Musique, les musiciens et les instruments de musique. Exposition Universelle de 1867*, Portier without date, p. 700. Cited in Dieterlen, *L'Harmonium* (see note 97), p. 478.
99. Cf. Maria Dunkel, *Bandoneon und Konzertina. Ein Beitrag zur Darstellung des Instrumententypus*, Munich & Salzburg 1987, p. 9.
100. Cf. Dieterlen, *L'Harmonium* (see note 97), p. 183.
101. Dunkel, *Harmonikainstrumente* (see note 96), col. 185.
102. Dieterlen, *L'Harmonium* (see note 97), p. 182.
103. The advertising material of Dwarkin & Sons (see note 17) refers explicitly to harmoniums "played by both hands and pedalled by legs sitting on a stool or chair", i.e. lap harmoniums were excluded.
104. Pratap Ghosh described a bellows system quite similar to that of the harmoniflûte [for the description, see Dunkel, *Harmonikainstrumente* (see note 96), col. 185.].
105. See *BINA Catalogue*, 2003.
106. Conversation with Vallabh Vidyanagar of Melvin Musicals, Gujarat, in September 2002.
107. See a.o. *BINA Catalogue*, 2003.
108. Information from Pratap Ghosh. Conversation on 16 May 2003.
109. Ord-Hume, letter (see note 9), p. 2.
110. Some harmonium players own a separate instrument for each singer they accompany regularly, e.g. Arawind Thatte.
111. Information from Pratap Ghosh (Dwarkin & Son, Kolkata, conversation on 16 May 2003) and Suphal and Suvoji Pakrashi (Pakrashi & Co., Kolkata, conversation on 17 May 2003).

112. Ord-Hume, letter (see note 9), p. 2.
113. Conversation with Vallabh Vidyanagar of Melvin Musicals, Gujarat, in September 2002.
114. Suphal and Suvoji Pakrashi (Pakrashi & Co., Kolkata, conversation on 17 May 2003).
115. Suphal and Suvoji Pakrashi (Pakrashi & Co., Kolkata, conversation on 17 May 2003). The combination of metals and the production methods remain company secrets and therefore were not revealed to me – even though the firm does not manufacture its own reeds, but buys them from other suppliers.
116. Reginald Byron (ed.), *Music, Culture, & Experience. Selected Papers of John Blacking*, Chicago 1995, p. 223.
117. Ananda Coomaraswamy, *The Dance of Shiva – Fourteen Indian Essays*, New York [1]1918, cited here from the issue Delhi 1999, *Essay Indian Music*, pp. 102–114, here p. 102.
118. Mark Levy, *Intonation in North Indian Music. A Select Comparison of Theories with Contemporary Practice*, Delhi 1982, p. 140.
119. Nazir Ali Jairazbhoy, *Sangeet Kala Vihar, English Supplement*, vol. 1 [incorporated into] *Journal of the Indian Musicological Society*, vols. 2–5, 1971–4. R.C. Mehta (ed.). Baroda: Jambu bet, Dandia Bazar (review), in: *Ethnomusicology* 19 (1975), pp. 316–318, here p. 317.
120. Panikkar, *Social Consciousness* (see note 27), p. 108.
121. This was by no means a singular phenomenon: Lata Mani writes e.g. about *sati*, widow immolation: "Tradition was not the ground on which the status of women was being contested. Rather the reverse was true: women in fact became the site on which tradition was debated and reformulated. What was at stake was not women but tradition." (Lata Mani, *Contentious Traditions: The Debate on Sati in Colonial India*, in: Kumkum Sangari & Sudesh Vaid (ed.), *Recasting Women*, Delhi 1989, p. 118, cited in: Panikkar, *Social Consciousness* (see note 27), p. 113). Mana's last sentence seems too rigid to me: surely it was about women, just not exclusively, similar to the case of harmonium – tradition.
122. Rabindranath Tagore, *Reminiscences*, in: *Sangeet Natak Academy Bulletin. Rabindranath Tagore Centenary Number*, Delhi 1961, p. 4.
123. Edward Said, *Orientalism*, New York [4]1995.
124. William Jones, *On the Musical Modes of the Hindus*, first published 1792, reprinted in Sourindo Mohan Tagore, *Hindu Music from Various Authors* (= Chowkhamba Sanskrit Studies, vol. XLIX), Varanasi 1965 [1875], pp. 125–160; Sir William Ousley (1767–1842), *Anecdotes of Indian Music*, reprinted in: Tagore, *Hindu Music* (as above), pp. 163–172; William C.

Stafford, *Oriental Music. The Music of Hindustan or India*, first published in 1830 and reprinted in: Tagore, *Hindu Music* (as above), pp. 218–228.

125. See e.g. Stafford, *Oriental Music* (see note 126), especially p. 219 et seq.
126. See e.g. P.T. French, *Catalogue of Indian Musical Instruments*, in: Tagore, *Hindu Music* (see note 126), pp. 244–273, here p. 269.
127. Terminology of Edgar Quinet, *Le Génie des religions*, in: *Œuvres complètes*, Paris 1857, pp. 55–74.
128. Reference to *West-Eastern Divan* shows that the phenomenon focussed not only on India – Persian and other texts received comparable attention.
129. Milton B. Singer, *When a Great Tradition Modernizes: An Anthropological Approach to Indian Civilization*, Chicago 1980, p. 27.
130. Said, *Orientalism* (see note 125), p. 79.
131. An overview of the supposed reasons for the demise of the musical tradition goes beyond the scope of this study. The Muslim Mogul-regime is often referred to in this context, which is a contradiction, seeing that this period also belongs to the so-called Golden Age of Indian music. This is a hotly debated part of Indian music history, and it still needs thorough investigation. General information on Muslim musical influence in India can be found in Regula Burckhardt Qureshi, *Sufi Music of India and Pakistan: Sound, Context and Meaning in Qawwali*, Chicago 1995.
132. A.H. Fox Strangways, *The Music of Hindostan*, Delhi [2]1994 [Oxford [1]1914], p. 15.
133. Said, *Orientalism* (see note 125), p. 79.
134. How the European perception of Indian literature developed is analysed vividly in Singer's classic text *A Passage to More than India: A Sketch of Changing European and American Images*, in: Singer, *Great Tradition* (see note 119), pp. 11–38. An interesting description of how the according (musical) perception of India is reflected in European music is provided by Jann Pasler, who looks at French music. Jann Pasler, *India and its Music in the French Imagination before 1913*, in: S.A.K. Durga (ed.), *Music: Intercultural Aspects. A Collection of Essays*, Mumbai & Baroda 1999, pp. 27–51.
135. On the role of the English language in Indian, British and Anglo-Indian musicology see Harold S. Powers, *Indian Music and the English Language: A Review Essay*, in: *Ethnomusicology* IX/1 (January 1965), pp. 1–12.
136. Fox Strangways, *The Music of Hindostan* (see note 134), p. 16.
137. Portrayed, albeit in a somewhat polarising manner, in: Said, *Orientalism* (see note 125), pp. 59–62.

138. The cliché of the Muslim rejection of music and the fine arts can be traced back to the Mogul emperor Aurangzeb; with Akbar before him the stark opposite attitude prevailed. On the Hindu perception of Muslims as a threat see Peter van der Veer, *Imperial Encounters*, Princeton 2001, p. 101 et seq.
139. N. Augustus Willard, *A Treatise on the Music of Hindoostan: Comprising a Detail of the Ancient Theory and Modern Practice*, Calcutta 1834; *Willard's Treatise on the Music of Hindustan*, in: *Journal of the Asiatic Society* 25, 1834.
140. Margaret E. Cousins, *India's Gift of Song*, in: Usha Sharma, *Heritage of Indian Music*, Jaipur 1996, vol. 2, pp. 179–187, here p. 185. The essay is an excerpt from Cousins, *The Music of the Orient and the Occident: Essays towards Mutual Understanding*, Madras 1935.
141. Fox Strangways, *The Music of Hindostan* (see note 134), p. 68.
142. Ibid., p. 163.
143. Ibid., p. 163 et seq.
144. E.g. ibid., p. 89 et seq.
145. Apart from the harmonisation of Indian music, a phenomenon, however, that he only encountered in European circles. Ibid., p. 164.
146. He goes as far as writing "of other lands" instead of his home country or Europe, as is by all means common in the terminology of the time.
147. Said, *Orientalism* (see note 125), p. 8.
148. Margaret E. Cousins, *The Music of the Orient and the Occident: Essays towards Mutual Understanding*, Madras 1935.
149. Margaret E. Cousins, *The Music of Hindustan*, in: Usha Sharma, *Heritage of Indian Music*, Jaipur 1996 vol. 1, p. 23. The essay is an excerpt from Cousins, *Music of the Orient and the Occident* (see note 142). The quotation above is on p. 28.
150. Ibid., p. 23.
151. Ibid., p. 256.
152. Ibid.
153. K.B. Deval, *The Hindu Musical Scale and the Twenty-Two Shrutees*, published 1910 (Summary in Ernest Clements, *Introduction to the Study of Indian Music*, Allahabad 1912); J.D. Paterson, *On the Gramas or Musical Scales of the Hindus*, reprinted in Tagore, *Hindu Music* (see note 126), p. 175–189 and many others.
154. Cousins, *Hindustan* (see note 151), p. 22.
155. Clements, *Study of Indian Music* (see note 155), p. 2.
156. Ibid.
157. Arthur W.J.G. Ord-Hume, *Harmonium: The History of the Reed Organ and Its Makers*, Vestal 1986, p. 156.

158. Napier, *Sangat* (see note 2), p. 131.
159. Thakur Jaideva Singh, *Indian Music*, Calcutta 1995, p. 475.
160. Gerry Farrell, *Indian Music and the West*, Oxford 1997, p. 52.
161. S.J. Sarkes, *A Treatise on the Similarities Between European and Indian Music*, Calcutta 1915, cited in Farell, *Indian Music and the West* (see note 154), p. 55.
162. Ernest Clements, *The Science of Intonation and the Theory of Indian Music*, in: *The Ragas of Hindusthan*, vol. 2, Poona 1921, p. 4.
163. Farell, *Indian Music* (see note 162), p. 55. For the exact Cent-values of the tuning system designed by him, see Levy, *Intonation* (see note 120), p. 111 et seq.
164. Napier, *Sangat* (see note 2), p. 131. Unfortunately there is no more information about the instrument, also not when it was built. Because Tembe was only born in 1881 and some of the European instruments were built even earlier, it seems likely that he was inspired by the European instruments.
165. Ord-Hume, *Harmonium* (see note 151), pp. 131 and 152.
166. Ibid., p. 155 et seq.
167. Ibid., p. 47.
168. Ibid., p. 132.
169 A comprehensive description of harmoniums as pure instruments is provided by Jobst P. Fricke, *Pitch bending und das Harmonium als Reininstrument. Mit einem Verzeichnis der Reininstrumente und deren Beschreibung*, in: Monika Lustig (ed.), *Harmonium und Handharmonika*, Blankenburg 2002, pp. 105–116.
170. Werner Lettermoser, *Hermann von Helmholz*, in: *Musik in Geschichte und Gegenwart 1*, Kassel et al. 1957, vol. 6, col. 127, Hans Heinz Dräger, *Paul von Janko*, in: *Musik in Geschichte und Gegenwart 1*, Kassel et al. 1957, vol. 6, col. 1711; Carl Dahlhaus, *Arthur Joachim von Oettingen*, in: *Musik in Geschichte und Gegenwart 1*, Kassel et al. 1957, vol. 9, col. 1891.
171. See Fricke, *Harmonium als Reininstrument* (see note 171), p. 105.
172. R.H.M. Bosanquet, *On the Hindu Division of the Octave, with Some Additions to the Theory of Systems of the Higher Orders*, in: *Proceedings of the Royal Society of London*, March–December 1877, reprinted in: Tagore, *Hindu Music* (see note 126), pp. 319–335.
173. *Shruti*-harmoniums are nevertheless propagated from time to time, and in the meantime mostly by Indians; mostly without much reaction. See Ram Jeevan Bhattacharya, *Shruti-Harmonium and Its Usefulness*, in: *Journal of the Sangeet Research Academy* vol. 14 (2000), pp. 21–25.

174. Bhavanrav A. Pingle, *Indian Music*, Delhi 1989 (first edition Kathiawar 1898), p. 29. I wish to thank Joep Bor for pointing me back to this source.
175. Ibid., p. 55; 155.
176. Ibid. p. 313.
177. Ibid., p. 297.
178. Tagore, *Reminiscences* (see note 124), p. 4. *My Reminiscences* was first published in 1917.
179. This letter from Tagore to Dwarkin, shown in figure 12, is from the archive of Dwarkin & Co., Calcutta; the original is in Bengal, the translation by Rohini Chowdhurry, London. Cleveland Johnson, in a paper read at the Conference India and the World: The Performing Arts, Amsterdam 20-22 November 2008, showed another advertisement of Dwarkin in which the same letter was quoted (but not shown). Curiously, Dwarkin & Co. in the latter ad attribute the letter to S.M. Tagore.
180. I am grateful for Joep Bor for the comment on Marris College.
181. E.g. Jonas Braasch & Gregor Klinke, *That Bane of Indian Music – Das Harmonium in Indien*, in: Monika Lustig (ed.), *Harmonium und Handharmonika. 20. Musikinstrumentenbau-Symposium Michaelstein, 19–21 November 1999*, Blankenburg 2002, pp. 83–100.
182. Banerjee, *Gita Sutra Sar* (see note 4), p. 32.
183. Ibid.
184. Ibid., p. 115.
185. Ibid., p. 116.
186. Ibid.
187. Babu Nanak Prasad, *Indian Music. Scientific and Practical*, Delhi [1906] 2003, p. 97.
188. Ibid.
189. Farrell, *Indian Music* (see note 162), p. 53.
190. Said, *Orientalism* (see note 125), p. 121.
191. A.I.R.; India has had radio since 1924, the name was changed to A.I.R. in 1936.
192. H.R. Luthra, *Indian Broadcasting*, Delhi 1986, p. 303.
193. I thank Joep Bor for pointing me to this important connection between the A.I.R. ban of the harmonium and that of the *baijis* and *tawaifs*. Also see Regula Burckhardt Qureshi, *How Does Music Mean? Embodied Memories and the Politics of Affect in the Indian "sarangi"*, in: American Ethnologist, Vol. 27, No. 4 (Nov. 2000), pp. 805-838, p. 825; K.S. Mullick, *Tangled Tapes: The Inside Story of Indian Broadcasting*, New Delhi 1974, p. 3.

194. The date varies in sources, 1950 is often stated erroneously; e.g. by Napier, *Sangat* (see note 2), p. 130.
195. See Neuman, *Life Of Music* (see note 77), p. 180 et seq.
196. See G.C. Awasthy, *Broadcasting in India*, Bombay et al. 1965, p. 37 et seq.
197. Also see Bob van der Linden, *Music, Theosophical spirituality, and empire: the British modernist composers Cyril Scott and John Foulds*, in: *Journal of Global History* 2008 (3), pp. 163-183.
198. Goswami, *Broadcasting: The New Patron of Indian Music*, Delhi 1996, p. 50.
199. Luthra, *Indian Broadcasting* (see note 194), p. 304.
200. Goswami, *Broadcasting* (see note 200), p. 50.
201. See ibid., p. 42 et seq.
202. Patanjali Maduskar, conversation on 8 April 2003, Mumbai.
203. Goswami, *Broadcasting* (see note 200), p. 52. The petition that finally led to the revision of the 1940 ban seems to have started its way from Pune: the harmonium player Appa Jalgaonkar seems to have spearheaded the initiative. Conversations with Vikas Kashalkar on 4 April 2003, Pune, and Appa Jalgaonkar on 7 April 2003, also in Pune.
204. Introduction to the symposium report, without mention of the author. In: *Journal of the Sangeet Natak Akademi* 20 (1971), p. 5.
205. P.V. Subramaniam, *The Harmonium in Light and Semi-Classical Music*, in: *Journal of the Sangeet Natak Akademi* 20 (1971), pp. 7–10, here p. 7.
206. S.N. Ratanjanker, *Harmonium and Indian Music*, in: *Journal of the Sangeet Natak Akademi* 20 (1971), pp. 11–14, here p. 11.
207. As stated by Deshpande [Vamanrao Hari Deshpande, *Harmonium as Accompaniment For Hindustani Classical Music*, in: *Journal of the Sangeet Natak Akademi* 20 (1971), pp. 15–19, here p. 16].
208. Addendum to the symposium report, in: *Journal of the Sangeet Natak Akademi* 20 (1971), p. 29.
209. Goswami, *Broadcasting* (see note 200), p. 51.
210. Vamanrao Hari Deshpande, *Harmonium as Accompaniment* (see note 209), p. 15.
211. Gayatri Chakravorty Spivak, *Can the Subaltern Speak?: Speculations on Widow Sacrifice*, in: *Wedge* 7 (8) (Winter/Spring) 1985, pp. 120–130, here p. 130.
212. David Kopf, *British Orientalism and the Bengali Renaissance: The Dynamics of Indian Modernization 1773–1835*, Berkeley 1969, p. 286.

As far a
departu
Chapte
its gen
sitting
impor
be cru
were t
centuri
Second
to a th
industr
The
of deb
most,
Indian

III.1.T

There
intonat
no clar

III

The Instrument

As far as its construction is concerned, the Indian harmonium's departure from its European predecessors is insignificant. (cf. Chapter II.2). Modifications to the instrument mostly involved its general ease of use (e.g. making it playable by someone sitting on the floor) or timbre (experiments with reeds) – important, yet unproblematic aspects. Another issue seems to be critical, though: the harmonium's tuning. Early harmoniums were usually tuned to equal temperament way into the 20th century, and this tuning system was only abandoned when the Second World War reduced the influx of European instruments to a trickle, making space for a burgeoning local harmonium industry.

The question as to which tuning is 'right' is still a matter of debate today and concerns the harmonium industry the most, seeing that the harmonium – contrary to most other Indian instruments – is unable to change its tuning ad hoc.

III.1. TUNING

There is a substantial amount of literature dealing with intonation and tuning in Northern Indian music, and it creates no clarity on the matter, stringing together diverse theories and interpretations. A representative overview of the situation as represented in the general literature is far beyond the scope of this book;[1] the final and binding answer to the question as to how the Indian octave is to be divided into intervals keeps posing a dilemma for Indian musicologists. In the context of the presumed close relationship of contemporary intonation practice with antiquity and its treatises on music (described in Chapter II.3.1) the scalar structures associated with Indian antiquity (especially as described in the *Natyashastra*) are often transferred to current musical practice, *i.e.* the latter is considered to be closely linked to its ancient roots. This is reflected by the relatively little significance that tends to be attributed to empirical audio analyses: because the ancient structures are prescriptive by nature, modern musical practice firstly is of secondary importance; secondly there is

> the belief among Indian scholars that an attempted empiricism is already implicit in the works of Bharata and other Sanskrit writers. Closely tied to this belief is the assumption that these ancient treatises are still relevant to modern performance practice, and that further empirical studies, therefore, would continue to substantiate traditional views.[2]

The ideal is fixed, therefore, and it is commonly expected that the prevalent practice follows this ideal. Accordingly, any discrepancies between measurements derived from contemporary performances and ancient theory may even be interpreted as nothing but evidence of a declining musical culture, – a musical predicament with little influence on "the tradition", however, which remains the ideal.

The according investigations – frequency analyses of singers and instrumentalists – are not only rare, but are usually conducted by European or Europe-oriented scholars; examples include the study of Deval and Clements,[3] the work done by Nazir Ali Jairazbhoy,[4] his student Mark Levy,[5] and Wim van der Meer.[6] The reliability of the investigations done by Clements and Deval has been questioned: they yielded measurements that are "too good to be true", as Harold Powers has pointed out.[7]

Common to all theories is that they do not accept equal temperament. Apart from that, the perspectives from which the harmonium is criticised for its (mostly) equal temperament are different. The fact that the concepts of dividing the octave into intervals diverge so strongly in my view also contributed to that the *shruti*-harmonium could not gain general acceptance, for only one scalar concept could be implemented at a time.

In the musicological discourse – be it the written or the more elusive oral discourse – the tonal system dictating current musical practice is sometimes theorised in a way that does not seem coherent. Measurements confirm that there apparently is no uniform frame of reference, or, if there is one, it is interpreted in different ways (although this flexibility is largely rejected and ascribed to minimal stylistic differences between *gharanas*, a claim that is untenable in the light of the measurements).[8] There is, therefore, an obvious discrepancy sometimes between what a musician says and what he does; the motivation for embedding an assumed theory into a superimposed context had been dealt with in previous chapters. For now our focus is on the analysis of the actual scales to which different harmoniums are tuned. This investigation is a lot less complicated than an analysis of the human voice, which varies pitches during the course of a *raga*. A lot of time is invested in tuning the harmonium; harmonium tuners and singers often work together on the fine-tuning, to ensure that the instrument corresponds to the singer's conception of the scale.[9]

III.1.1 Measurements, Tuning, Intonation

The most common tuning system for the harmonium is the so-called Indian Standard Tuning. This name is somewhat misleading, since it mainly refers to a tuning system that does not correspond to equal temperament. This, my interlocutors said, is either the so-called *gandhar*-tuning (which corresponds to natural tuning), or an equally tempered scale with slightly lowered third step (Ga) – therefore a hybrid between pure and tempered tuning. The latter is no "standard" tuning, since "slightly lowered" is open to interpretation and harmoniums are tuned by ear. Also, Jairazbhoy points out that harmoniums are mostly tuned to the singer's notion: "These only approximate to a twelve semitone standard."[10]

Levy has proven empirically that the intonation of the human voice is handled along similar lines: for each step in the scale there is a certain bandwidth within which the intonation of the voice still sounds correct. According to Levy's data the upper and lower limits of this bandwidth can be as much as 50 Cent apart within one performance.[11] The singer's intonation of specific scale degrees is influenced decisively by the melodic context.

To find out how the harmonium with its fixed pitches fits into the context of this vocal flexibility, the tuning of two harmoniums were investigated with frequency analysis.[12] The manufacturers of both instruments stated that the instruments were tuned by ear to a pure tuning system. The results are shown concisely in tables and graphs in the Appendix.

The results show that the harmoniums are on no account tuned to a natural scale, but that the tuning orients itself to the equally tempered scale.[13] The average deviation from the latter is 5 Cent; even if Alexander Ellis calls such a deviation easily recognisable,[14] experience made with frequency analysis in the field of musicology[15] shows that such a discrepancy is almost irrelevant and that it can also be "made to fit" by the listener when it is embedded in a musical/functional context.[16]

There obviously is no systematic connection between the deviations in the first and second octaves. All discrepancies are within the tolerance range for equal temperament also common in European tuning systems (cf. the measurements in the Appendix).

The use of tempered instruments like the investigated harmoniums reconfirm that tempered tuning is used in North Indian classical music.

> Differing intonation in the various ragas is not such a vital part of North Indian classical music to-day. We do not mean that [...] the Western scale prevails in India but that the Western tempered scale is within the tolerance allowed in the intonation of the various notes of the scales commonly used in north Indian classical music.[17]

By this Nazir Jairazbhoy obviously does not mean that tuning is handled arbitrarily, but postulates an inherent flexibility in intonation. The question remains whether this applies as universally as he suggests, *i.e.* for all the musicians in a given ensemble. With reference to Chapter IV.2.2 the possibility has to be considered that only the player of the accompanying melodic instrument is granted such "musical crudities", while the soloist is expected to adhere to a subtle and strict system of intonation through training. This corresponds to the singers" perception, who almost exclusively would not admit that they are influenced in their conception of intonation by the harmonium's accompaniment. Mark Levy's research yielded another insight – that the same singer shows very strong deviations in intonation, and sometimes sings more tempered or more purely, depending on the melodic accompaniment he has. His data seems to indicate that the trend in Indian music is moving towards tempered tuning; it also proves, however, that the harmonium's fixed tuning does not curb the degree of flexibility necessary for such a development.[18]

In this context it seems clear that the decisive reason for the harmonium's use is the singer's superiority compared to the instrument, an aspect that has only gained in relevance recently (cf. Chapter IV.2.2). That singers adapt their intonation to the current musical context is also necessary and has been proved: "Notes tended to be higher in pitch in ascending melodic lines or when associated with higher notes in general."[19] On the other hand the harmonium's fixed tuning prohibits any functional emphasis of leading notes by means of a change in intonation.

What seems to make the harmonium a problematic instrument for Indian music, given the singer's variable intonation, is not the potential influence on the singer and the resulting "corruption" of the *raga*: the equal temperament of the harmonium seems to be at extreme odds with the *tanpuras*, an essential part of North Indian classical music ensembles. Especially the clash of the harmonium's tempered third with the *tanpura*'s natural third is problematic, even if it may be weakened by the fact that *tanpura* as well as harmonium operate in the background.

The analysis of the actual tuning of harmoniums yields a fundamental paradox of North Indian music: "No consistent correlations were observed [...] between the measured pitches and any single theoretical system".[20] "My interlocutors as well as the literature rejected empirically proved facts in favour of an assumed ideal, which is projected onto musical reality. The actual paradox is not between the perceived shortcomings of the harmonium and its use in Indian music, but, in terms of intonation, the divergence between partially ideologised theories and musical reality.

III.1.2 Timbre

As mentioned earlier, the European free reeds were developed early on with a timbral conception that was oriented towards the human voice. The timbral kinship of harmonium and human voice is nowhere as obvious as in Indian music; already Krishna Dhan Banerjee, writing in 1886, mentions the instrument's scope of timbre.[21] If early harmoniums were often regarded as having a certain coarseness and hoarseness, all musicians I talked to agreed without exception that the "modern" harmonium comes very close to the vocal sound.

Those singers using the harmonium also lauded its ability to adapt its timbre through the basic choice of reeds and the combination of stops. The combination of stops does not refer to the changing of stops during performance, for within the performance of a single piece a change of couplers is extremely rare;[22] what is rather meant is that the sound is adapted to fit the range of the voice, which is done stereotypically: the three sets of reeds a harmonium usually has are called *kharaj* ("bass"), *nar* ("masculine") and *madi* ("feminine"); which refers primarily to the pitch and therefore to the rank of the respective set. Accordingly, a sonorous male voice is accompanied with *kharaj*, while a softer voice is accompanied with the *nar*-stop and, if necessary, with a coupled *kharaj*- or *madi*-stop. A female voice is usually accompanied with the combination *nar*- and *madi*-stops.

Because every singer has his own Sa (*i.e.* his own voice determines the modal system's tonic, usually between C' and E-flat') the harmonium is tuned to the according pitch. With a *sarangi* – or any other stringed instrument – a scordatura would always mean a change in timbre, even if slight.

In Indian music the ideal singing voice has a natural vocal sound; by adapting the instrument to the current register of the voice this natural quality can be enhanced, because the singer does not have to go to vocal extremes to adapt to his accompaniment. This affects the vocal timbre, because the singer does not need to press his voice, for instance, to sing extremely high notes.

Because every singer usually owns a harmonium, or sings regularly with an accompanist who owns a harmonium adapted to his voice, a high level of blending is possible between instrumental and vocal sound.

If the *sarangi* is said to come closest to imitating the human voice,[23] then this rather vague statement can only refer to an area other than timbre; still, when asked, some of the musicians stated that the timbre is meant, without giving any details or reasons.[24] In my opinion the *sarangi's* decisive ability that would justify such a statement would be its ability to express emotion: it can produce vocal colourations of almost every kind, very closely resembling that of the human voice, yet its actual timbre does not come especially close to that of the human voice.

The harmonium's superior ability to create a homogeneously blended sound together with the human voice, therefore, is preferred to the *sarangi's* superior ability to imitate the more subtle vocal affects. Musically these are two entirely independent areas; accordingly the choice does not mean that one of these areas is rejected. A soloist has to make a choice according to his personal preferences, and this decision is complicated by many other considerations concerning the instrument (e.g. intonation).

Excursion: Volume

An instrument's volume potential is another facet of the timbral aspect, and this not because of systematic,

> but because of comparative reasons. As with timbre, the soloist's choice for the harmonium and its louder volume is not made absolutely, but in consideration of the other possibilities. The argument of the harmonium's greater volume was very important during the late 19th and early 20th century, because PA systems only spread slowly due to a number of reasons. Simultaneously the audiences grew larger, which meant that unamplified performances had to fill bigger venues. This posed less of a problem for the singer: vocal soloists who had received their training before microphones were common are said to have had a much greater dynamic range than those trained thereafter. It was rather the accompanying instruments that had to become more widely audible – which clearly means that the accompanying instrument was not restricted to supporting the singer, but that it by all means had musical functions. For this none of the established instruments was appropriate,[25] so that the harmonium was superior in this respect.

After the harmonium and PA-technology had established themselves, the singing technique changed fundamentally. A comparison of historic and modern recordings makes clear that singers, freed from the need to fill larger venues (or more seldom, to perform at open air concerts), could concentrate on their vocal timbre and technique.[26] It seems likely that the use of the harmonium (which is unable to reproduce these fine vocal nuances) is a consequence from this development, to the point of emphasising the subtleness of the singer's voice. Yet this is based not purely on musical considerations, but especially on social aspects regarding ensemble playing in modern India.

Endnotes

1. For a discussion of intonation issues and scales, see Wim van der Meer, *Hindustani Music in the Twentieth Century,* The Hague 1981, p. 8 et seq.
2. Levy, *Intonation* (see note 120), p. 1 et seq.
3. Deval/Clements [Clements, *Introduction* (see note 155); *Lectures on Indian Music*, Bombay 1927] at no point show how they gained their information. The recordings also were made especially for the purpose of pitch analysis; the musicians' (among others Abdul Karim Khan) attention were therefore drawn to this point, which makes the recordings not representative but influenced.
4. Levy, *Intonation* (see note 120), pp. 119–132.
5. Ibid.
6. Meer, *Hindustani Music* (see note 213).
7. Harold S. Powers, *Review Essay* (see note 137), p. 4.
8. Cf. especially the results of Levy, *Intonation* (see note 120).
9. Conversation with Sanjeev Abhyankar, on 3 April 2003 in Pune. With the "singer's conception of the scale" the *Gharana* specific characteristics are meant.
10. Nazir Ali Jairazbhoy, *The Ragas of North Indian Music*, London 1971, p. 34.
11. Levy, *Intonation* (see note 120), p. 95 et seq.
12. The pitch analysis was done using the Algorhythm "YIN" [Alain de Cheveigné und Hideki Kawahara, *YIN, a fundamental frequency estimator for speech and music*, in: Journal of the Acoustical Society of America vol. 111 (2002), pp. 1917–1930] under the programming language Matlab 6.1. I am thankful to Jonas Braasch for conducting some of the frequency analyses.
13. The measurements therefore confirm the results of Braasch & Klinke (see note 183).
14. Alexander J. Ellis, *On the Musical Scales of Various Nations*, in: *Journal of the Society of the Arts*, vol. XXXIII (27 March 1885).
15. See e.g. B. Frans Fransson, Johan Sundberg & Per Tjernlund, *The Scale in Played Music*, in: *Svensk tidskrift för musikforskning* 56:1 (1974), pp. 49–54.
16. Cf. Christian Ahrens' research into the intonation of a Greek klarino-player. Christian Ahrens, *Ein griechischer Volksmusiker und sein Instrument. Zur Stimmung folkloristischer Aerophone*, in: Erich Stockmann (ed.), *Studia Instrumentorum Musicae Popularis VII*, Stockholm 1981, pp. 95–101.
17. Nazir Ali Jairazbhoy & W.A. Stone, *Intonation in Present-Day in North Indian Classical Music*, in: *Bulletin of the School of Oriental and African Studies* University of London vol. XXVI (1963), pp. 119–132, here p. 129.

18. Levy, *Intonation* (see note 120), especially tables 13–16. For the conclusion mentioned last one has to take into consideration which accompanying instruments are playing on the recordings.
19. Levy, *Intonation* (see note 120), p. 142.
20. Levy, *Intonation* (see note 120), p. 142.
21. Banerjee, *Gita Sutra Sar* (see note 4), p. 31.
22. An exception is the recording of Bhairav by Vijay Kichlu and the harmonium player Jyoti Goho. Goho, whose personal style can indeed be called progressive and unique – the intensive use of chords has already been mentioned – applies this effect only once, and for a very short time. See the transcription in Napier, *Sangat* (see note 2), vol. II, p. 517 et seq.
23. This thesis was early on introduced in the written discourse. See e.g. François Baltazard Solvyns, *Les Hindôus*, Paris 1810, vol. II, nr. 7 (3).
24. E.g. Panatjali Maduskar, on 8 April 2003. After several conversations with musicians it became clear that certain theorems (like the one concerning the similarity of *sarangi* and vocal timbre) are repeated without reflection. Veena Sahasrabuddhe, who eyes theorems very critically, was the only one to emphasise that the harmonium's timbre comes closest to the human voice by far. Conversation on 7 April 2003, Mumbai.
25. Only the *shahnai* would have matched or surpassed the volume of the harmonium. But such a difference in timbre would have entailed a fundamental change in the character of accompaniment. To this day an accompanying *shahnai* is only used in combination with a solistic *shahnai*.
26. This phenomenon can be found in an almost identical form in other music traditions, e.g. the Arabic music tradition. For the Indian tradition also Prabha Atre (born in 1932) confirms: "Before the microphone arrived on the scene, a voice which could be heard in the farthest corner of a hall was considered good. Naturally, the artistic work on the notes had to be such that it could be heard by all. Volume of voice being an essential feature, the notes tended to be straight and bold [...] The microphone brought about a revolution in music. Audibility was no longer a problem; even a breath could be heard in amplification. The tonal quality of sound assumed great importance. The artist began [!] to think in terms of making conscious use of volume, timbre, range and speed to increase the communicative capacity of his voice." Prabha Atre, *Modernity in Khyal: ome Notes*, in: *Sangeet Natak – Journal of the Sangeet Natak Akademi* 89–90 (July–December 1988). Special Issue on Tradition and Modernity, pp. 16–23, here p. 19.

IV

Musical Use

All India Radio's solomonic decision to accept the harmonium as an accompanying but not solistic instrument was not beyond dispute. To this day, musicians express contradicting opinions regarding the instrument's potential: some of my informants drew upon the same argument to arrive at opposite stances towards the harmonium as a solo- and accompanying instrument respectively. The uncertainty in this matter seems to be based on the lack of agreement whether the solo or the accompanying function is the more challenging in Indian music. Some argue that during accompaniment the proximity to the vocals emphasises the harmonium's shortcomings because what the singer does will never be achieved on the harmonium. If an instrument is considered unsuitable for solistic purposes, but apt for melodic accompaniment, and if at the same time certain flaws can be tolerated in the one area, but not in another, then it is most obvious that there are diverging ideas concerning the aesthetic requirements made by the various musical functions in one and the same musical system. This points to the fundamental, but unsettled, question at the core of this paradox situation: what is the function of an accompanying instrument in Indian music and of melodic accompaniment itself, after all?[1] In which way do accompanying and solistic styles differ in harmonium playing? If harmonium players regard certain characteristics of the instrument as a weakness, which strategies do they develop to compensate for it? Are these techniques different in accompaniment and solistic function? How effective are they? The strategies that harmonium accompanists employ in order to live up to the standards of melodic accompaniment are discussed in a subsequent section (IV.2); to begin with, an examination of recordings will serve to point out tangible differences between current practices of solo singing and harmonium playing respectively.

IV.1 THE HARMONIUM AS SOLO INSTRUMENT

In concerts as well as on recordings, the number of harmonium solos is small compared to those of other solo instruments. This is due to the controversial character of the genre; yet harmonium solos are by no means curiosities anymore.

According to their own statements, most harmonium soloists use instruments with just intonation rather than tempered tuning. Those who use instruments with tempered tuning are mostly members of the older generation of harmonium players who were musically most active in the first half of the twentieth century, such as Appa Jalgaonkar.[2]

The *raga* repertoire of harmonium soloists is generally confined to "unproblematic" *ragas*, i.e. to those in which the essential characteristics and ornaments (*alankara*) do not confront the musician with problems of execution, such as *ragas* that demand e.g. an *andolan* on particular scale degrees (for example, *raga Darbari Kanada*), or *ragas* with tonal architecture that requires the rendition of discrete scale degrees such as *ati komal* or the like (for example *raga Miyan Mallar*).[3] Obviously, this considerably diminishes the *raga* repertoire of the genre.

As far as the overall form of a harmonium solo is concerned, the options available to the musician are similar to those of any other soloist: the two most popular forms are (1) the sequence *alap – jor – jhala – gat – tan*, and (2) the imitation of the *khyal* form.

Direct comparison: harmonium solo, vocal solo

In order to demonstrate differences between the respective *raga* interpretations of harmonium soloists and vocalists, I shall briefly compare the beginning of two *alap*s. Both are in *raga Maru Bihag*, and they are performed by *khyal* singer Shruti Sadolikar[4] and harmonium soloist Arawind Thatte, respectively.[5]

There is a big difference between the two interpretations as far as the overall conception is concerned. They differ in duration: Sadolikar's performance lasts 3'53", Thatte's harmonium solo 35'. In both cases, I shall look at the immediate beginning in order to compare aspects of the technical, rather than the formal, rendition of the *raga Maru Bihag*.

The difficulties usually involved with the transcription of music play a critical role here: articulation and ornaments cannot be adequately represented with conventional notation systems, and those are the elements of the performance that are exceptionally important. For this reason the main objects of examination are the audio examples; the notation only serves as an orientation. The rhythmic structure can be – and should be, regarding the improvisational character of the *alap*[6] and the Indian notation customs – notated in its rough contours only.

A visual comparison of the two transcriptions already shows a fundamental difference: while Thatte (music example 1[7]) frequently employs ornaments enveloping main pitches,

Sadolikar confines herself to acciaccaturas and upper mordents (at the beginning of the third phrase, see the transcription).[8] Yet applying the term "upper mordent" and its notation is misleading in this case: the recording shows that it is a *kan*, an ornament that corresponds most closely with the European upper mordent, yet is executed much more smoothly due to the vocal sound and is closer to a small glissando. This visually distinct difference corresponds to the aurally most prominent difference between the two recordings: Sadolikar's performance is characterised by *minds* and a rather streaming pitch progression that is characterised by glissandi, which emphasises the musical flow.

Contrasting this vocal sound with its characteristic and very subtle voice inflections, Thatte, on the other hand, proposes a *raga* conception which accentuates the single note, *i.e.* scale degree, even when it is embedded in virtuoso ornaments. This increases the *raga's* transparency, 'academicising' the listening process to a certain extent.

Ex. 1: Arawind Thatte playing *raga* Maru Bihag, transcription of the beginning of the *alap* section.

Within his intensive use of ornaments in this early stage of the *alap*, Thatte employs ornaments which are usually featured in this density only in the subsequent formal units of instrumental and vocal forms [see, for instance, the *khatka* (S F R S F S) in the last line)]. In my opinion he attempts to compensate the harmonium's stable, non-dynamic sound quality by using such "subtleties", instead of merely emulating the complexity and versatility of the human voice.

This is, first and foremost, due to the harmonium's particular possibilities and limitations. A *raga* interpretation that focuses on scale degree is sensible when it is simply impossible to work with the techniques that over centuries have been developed to make the most of one particular sound medium, the human voice: for instance, the floating, glissando-like pitch movement. On the other hand, the vocal sound is the undisputed ideal of Indian music, which makes Thatte's solution remarkable, precisely because he does not try to emulate this model. On the contrary, he tries to substitute those details that are particularly difficult or even impossible to realise on the harmonium – *mind* and *andolan*, for instance – with alternatives that, in his eyes, do justice to the peculiarities of the harmonium. Only in places does he overlap two pitches (see music example 1, third and fifth lines) in order to execute an ornament resembling a *mind*. In doing so, he is acting rather progressively, regarding the context of the Indian music system: by modifying the aesthetic principles very slightly, he offers an alternative that is on an equal footing with the omnipresent ideal of the human voice.

Other instrumentalists generally acknowledge the leading role that singers play.[9] Thatte himself regards the matter pragmatically:

> I am trying to make the most out of it, but there are certain things which I cannot do on the harmonium

> [...] But there are so many patterns that can be produced on my instrument and that cannot be produced by any other instrument or by the voice. So I should focus on that. That will be my potential. I will look at it positively. Not negatively.[10]

For Thatte, the harmonium is a new resource for Indian classical music, and he exploits the inherent flexibility of the musical system: "No pattern is vitally necessary. If you cannot produce a pattern, you should work on the other lines. Try to hide the negative points, then you can produce good music on the harmonium also."[11] This statement already hints at what Thatte himself states later on: for Indian music, the harmonium is a compromise. For him, the reason for adopting the harmonium as his primary medium of expression, even though he has received training in singing, is the attractive timbre of the harmonium.

There is a second complex of problems that Thatte's recording points to: the instrument's tuning. Like many contemporary musicians, Thatte considers just intonation to be the one authoritative tuning for Indian music. For this reason, he says, his harmonium was tuned to just intonation. In comparison with tempered tuning, the character of leading notes appears decisively altered in just intonation; this will be discussed in a separate chapter of this study.

There are also parallels between the practices prevalent in solo singing and harmonium playing. These similarities also occur in places where a difference in vocal practice would have been expected: for instance in the realm of phrasing. Thatte's phrasings last fifteen to twenty seconds at most, a duration which corresponds to the longest phrase sung before the singer has to breathe. In other instrumental performances – for instance on *sitar* or *sarod* – longer phrases are by all means built up. And while Thatte otherwise rejects the unassailable primacy of the human voice, this shows that the harmonium as solo instrument does stand closer to the voice than to other instruments, or that the musical form of singing, rather than another instrumental form, has been the starting point and inspiration for the relatively young genre of harmonium solo.

Thatte's personal style lies at one end of a spectrum, at the other end of which there are nearly contrary styles: styles which unambiguously try to imitate the vocal sound and the capabilities of the human voice (the heavy usage of glissandos, in particular).

Solistic use of the harmonium is hardly a recent phenomenon, quite to the contrary; but it is not an established part of musical life either. For this reason, the genre is still comparatively open and perhaps more ready to explore new ground than established genres. The strategies by which the harmonium's 'limitations' are being compensated in solo performance are identical to those that are generally being employed in accompaniment (see below); the various styles basically differ in when and how they tend to apply these techniques. This is a matter of aesthetics rather than one of mere technically viable options. The strategies, therefore, do not change with their functional context; rather they are similar in accompanying and solistic function. The following subchapter will provide concrete examples for this.

The question of whether the harmonium is capable of performing every *raga* has been answered differently, as the A.I.R. referendum had shown. The musicians considering the harmonium suitable for use in any *raga* are a small minority. They are mostly active harmonium soloists themselves, and they regard just intonation as prerequisite for such unlimited suitability.

These differences are based on two crucial points: (1) what are the indispensable components of a *raga*, and are ornaments such as *mind* among them? (2) can the harmonium actually produce the ornaments that are hard to realise on a keyboard (*mind, gamak, andolan*, to name but a few), or can musicians only try to come as close as possible to the unachievable ideal? If a musician reckons that the harmonium is indeed able to produce any ornament, question (1) becomes irrelevant. There is, however, general agreement that this is not the case,[12] and that imitations do not live up to the original ornaments. The fact that most harmonium soloists also agree with this throws an interesting light on the underlying concept of *raga*. Arawind Thatte expresses the generally accepted view that Indian concert-goers have a comparatively high standard of education: they are connoisseurs. This audience, according to Thatte, has, to varying degrees, a clearly defined idea of the ideal *raga* performance; Indian listeners, he goes on, are capable of compensating for an imperfect *raga* rendition by blending their individual notion of the *raga* in question and the actually heard sound into a satisfactory, or even very good, aural experience.[13] In my opinion, this is an optimistic interpretation of reality. Even if the Indian audience does possess an exceptionally high degree of connoisseurship, harmonium solo is not (yet) a genre that caters to this particular group of listeners. It seems to me rather that the flexibility inherent in any *raga* performance – which is historically manifest in the complexity of the *gharana* system – makes room for what a harmonium solo inevitably entails: either a clear stylistic change or an approximate solution. Given the history of Indian music, particularly the rapid pace of change in the last centuries, it seems likely that this flexibility has become ubiquitous enough during the last century to make it possible for the harmonium to be accepted as a solo instrument.

In any case, advocates of the harmonium conditionally accept an imperfect *raga* rendition, the condition being that the shortcomings of the harmonium are taken into account. Whether the listeners can always point out these drawbacks in a given performance, and whether they could do so to a lesser or a greater extent in the early days of the harmonium in India, is an entirely different question.

IV.2 The Harmonium Accompanying Vocals

Since the beginning of the second half of the twentieth century, the harmonium has been the instrument used most often to accompany singers.[14]

The following section explores the strategies that harmonium accompanists have developed to turn their much-criticised instrument into a suitable medium of melodic accompaniment. The aim is not to examine the emergence and development or the general role and function of the accompanying instrument;[15] instead the following questions are asked: Which musical techniques are employed to compensate the harmonium's inability to execute a certain ornament demanded by the piece he is accompanying? Which strategies are developed in 'collaboration' with the singer to ameliorate or at least avoid the limitations of the instrument? An examination of recordings of selected ornaments which are especially relevant to the vocal style provides answers. No attempt is made to judge how convincing the respective techniques are; the singers' general acceptance is sufficient judgement. Representing the opinion of most singers accompanied by harmoniums, Veena Sahasrabuddhe says: "For all these [ornaments], my harmonium player has a satisfactory answer; there are techniques."[16]

IV.2.1 Ornaments

If asked for the function of the accompanying instrument, an Indian musician is likely to respond: "An accompanying instrument is supposed to shadow the human voice." This formulation has nearly become a lexical expression; the accompanying instrument is supposed to follow the solo voice as closely as possible, without rivalling it. The intended overall sound ideal is an imitative heterophony between subordinate accompanist and instructive singing voice. The accompanying instrument is, moreover, supposed to "fill in" breathing and other pauses of the singer, thus bridging short periods of time by means of musical ideas that have been provided earlier in the piece by the soloist. When a harmonium is being used, the critical point in this dependency of accompanist on soloist is that technically, the soloist's "master pattern" and the accompanist's reproduction thereof have to be rendered in quick succession. This is crucial only when the musical detail in question is a key element of the respective *raga* that is being performed; otherwise, musical freedom provides ample space for the musician to revert to musical alternatives. In case the melodic idea that is to be imitated by the accompanist is particularly challenging for the harmonium and cannot be imitated faithfully, the temporal proximity of the ideal (vocal) original and the possibly imperfect (harmonium) copy might reinforce the notion that the harmonium is perhaps not the ideal solution. The popularity and intensive use of the harmonium, however, contradict this inference; on the contrary, the appreciation that it receives suggests that measured by its function, the harmonium's capabilities are satisfactory, and the instrument contributes to the flow of a *raga* performance. This means that harmonium players must have found effective ways to overcome black-and-white contrasts such as suitable-unsuitable by finding musical compromises.

There are several other musical instruments that are being used in contemporary India that pose comparable challenges. If they have mostly been imported rather than developed solely on Indian soil, they do not all derive from the European cultural area: the guitar, the saxophone and others come to mind, but particularly the *santur*, and in a sense also the *sitar*, which in recent centuries advanced to being one of the main instruments of Indian solo music. In the case of the *sitar*, the difficulties that had to be overcome were less obtrusive, but the situation with the *santur* is directly comparable to that of the harmonium. The tendency to musically exploit an imported musical instrument's potential by taking it further than this had commonly been done in the originating culture, thus, is evident not only in connection with the harmonium.

IV.2.1.a *Gamaka*

The *gamaka* does not have an equivalent in Euro-American music. "Musical notes are so produced as to touch upon the lower as well as the upper adjacent notes by resorting to a vibratory mode of vocalizing."[17] It is a specifically vocal sound, the reproduction of which is critical on most musical instruments: it is produced by a very fast back-and-forth oscillation between lower and upper pitch, during which the diaphragm rhythmically contracts and relaxes. An alternative could be a trill or other ornaments that center around the central pitch.

In music example 2,[18] the execution of a *gamaka* by a *sarangi* and a harmonium, respectively, are compared. Both instruments are played simultaneously and interact, yet the ornament's execution is not influenced by this – in a performance with only one of either instruments the ornament can be played like this again. The accompanying recording shows clearly that the *sarangi* follows the singer much more closely than the harmonium.

Ex. 2: Direct comparison of *gamaka* execution by a *sarangi* (middle system) and harmonium (lowest system). Transcription by John Napier.

It is obvious that the *sarangi* part resembles the vocal template much more closely: the *sarangi* indeed "shadows" the voice, and since the *gamaka* effect can be emulated fairly well on a *sarangi*, reproduction is not a problem at all. The harmonium player, on the other hand, cannot alter the pitch of the sound that he is producing, once he has struck a key. Therefore, there is no way for him to inflect pitch, let alone steplessly glide back and forth between two pitches. Instead, he employs appoggiaturas and quick returning notes in order to demarcate the narrow framework of the tonal spectrum that he is covering. By subdividing beats into rhythmic units that are partly syncopic to, and interlocking with, the *sarangi's* melodic line, he thickens the heterophonic musical texture and at the same time intertwines the harmonium's part with the remaining parts. In doing so, he in one aspect achieves an overall effect that is not too far from that of the vocal line's *gamaka*: rather than proposing a horizontal melodic line, he seems to produce a sound band, saturating the overall musical texture.

The immediate listening impression, though, is different, for the aural difference between a glide between two pitches and their rapid repetition cannot be resolved. While aurally, then, there remains an audible difference between the harmonium's part, on the one hand, and the soloist's and the *sarangi's* part on the other, and while the techniques employed respectively are necessarily of a differing nature in either case, both try to achieve the same effect musically. Here, the harmonium player cannot imitate the original sound pattern, but he does provide a musical unit that is musically and structurally in just the same line as the model pattern.

IV.2.1.b *Andolan*

The *andolan* is a slow oscillation on a distinct pitch. This ornament is particularly hard to imitate on a keyboard instrument, also because it mostly incorporates microtonal scale degrees. Recognising this, many harmonium players abstain from trying to find a substitute for it and revert to a completely different musical phrase as replacement, as in music example 3,[19] which stems from a transcription of an interpretation of *raga Bhairav*. A constitutive element of *Bhairav* is the *andolan* on *vadi* and *samvadi*, *dha* and *re,* respectively. Here, harmonium accompanist Jyoti Goho replaces the *andolan* with the dissonance of the simultaneously held pitches *Sa*, *Ma* and *Pa*. In this particular example, there are two 'reasons' for the insertion of a dissonance: as *samvadi* in *Bhairav*, *Re* is a scale degree which receives particular emphasis, and at the same time, it demands an *andolan*. An alternative technique that is sometimes being utilised in such a case is the quick turn around the pitch that carries the *andolan*; the lack of several ornaments is compensated for this way.

Ex. 3: Compensation of an *andolan* by means of chords. Harmonium (lower system) and voice (upper system). Transcription by John Napier.

IV.2.1.c *Mind*

The term *mind* describes a large variety of glissandos between two pitches. In a strict sense, it designates a glissando executed very slowly; other, more rapidly sung forms are designated by their own technical terms. The melodic shapes of these glissandos can assume various forms: commencing immediately after, shortly after, or long after starting the pitch of departure, and may lead to the target pitch by touching on inserted "resting points" on the way, or not. Wim van der Meer has provided a graphic illustration of some of the possible varieties.[20] Each of these varieties – and countless other possibilities – carry a distinct semantic meaning,[21] and it is obvious that the harmonium cannot produce these subtle nuances the way the vocal tract can. Therefore, the harmonium player can only aim at a more general, less differentiated, reproduction of decreased functional significance: the musical meaning is reduced.

Conceptually, a *mind* touches upon every *shruti* that lies between the starting pitch and the target pitch. This implies that a tonal inventory is employed that is not commonly part of the respective *raga*; harmonium players, therefore, in places insert pitches, or strike keys that are technically extrinsic to the respective *raga*. However, they never revert to a common and suggestive technique of the Euro-American region, running over the keys with the backs of their fingers or thumb, probably not least because this technique does not comply with the demand to touch on literally all *shrutis* in between two given pitches. Instead, they employ other methods, according to the musical context:

(1) Simultaneously striking two or even more pitches that are adjacent, or, at least close to each other, produces a sound that is reminiscent of "something like a *mind*".[22] This technique is chosen depending on the given intervallic frame: If only

two pitches are being produced at a time, the interval generally does not exceed a fourth; in case of pitch distances that transcend a fourth, harmonium players tend to produce a tone cluster by holding several (adjacent) pitches at a time.

(2) If the framing interval is relatively large, for instance, a seventh or an octave, harmonium players often react with a solution that far from emulates the glissando sound of the *mind*: they fill the intervallic gap with a small, sometimes rhythmically simple, motive which has a clear tendency up- or downwards. This is not an attempt to copy the phenomenon *mind*. Music example 4 shows such a replication by the harmonium that commences once that vocal soloist has reached the destination pitch (f^1):[23]

Ex. 4: *Mind* imitation by filling the intervallic 'gap'. The vocal part is notated in the upper, the harmonium part in the lower line. Transcription by John Napier.

(3) Sometimes harmonium accompanists simply ignore the *mind*. If, for instance, the harmonium player "follows" the soloist closely, the target pitch is anticipated, omitting the *mind*, and "landing" on the glissando's target pitch together with the vocalist. Because of the quick succession of events it can hardly be noticed that the *mind* is left out.

(4) If the *mind* is of lesser functional meaning, harmonium players sometimes plainly signify that the final pitch is

approached from below (in the case of an upward glide) or from above (in the case of a downward glide), for instance by having a mordent or simple trill precede the target pitch.

IV.2.1.d *Other techniques*

Non-tempered intervals

Several *ragas* require pitches that are *ati komal* or *tivratar*: "lower" or "higher" in intonation when compared to the reference scale degree. Regardless of an instrument's tuning, such pitches are not provided for on a normal keyboard. Since they cannot be produced correctly on a keyboard instrument, these critical scale degrees have to be avoided in some way or other. In many *ragas*, however, these scale degrees are central to the *raga's* structure, making the consequent omission of the respective scale degree undesirable. In such cases, harmonium players often revert to the cluster technique that has been described in IV.2.1.c; sometimes, moreover, they emphasise this process by a short increase of bellow pressure, regardless of whether the respective pitch needs to be raised or lowered. The objective is not to alter the pitch; it rather seems that the dynamic effect is employed to distract the listener's attention from the pitch.

Excursus: multi-pitch sounds and chords

> The usage of multi-pitch sounds and chords in Indian music is a development of the twentieth century, and it has not yet been examined systematically. In harmonium accompaniment of classical genres, they do not exclusively occur in connection with a *mind*, which means that they serve various purposes. Dissonant chords often serve to disguise a certain ornament that is associated with a particular scale

degree. In addition to this, they may also act to emphasise particular scale degrees: mostly the *vadi*, but in places also the *samvadi*.

In the "lighter" genres of *thumri* and *ghazal*, chords often have a harmonic function – a Euro-American influence which most likely coming from the genre of Bollywood songs –, but this is not or only exceptionally the case in *khyal*. The introduction of chordal harmony can certainly be traced back to the possibilities the harmonium offered. Although the guitar is also used in Indian music (especially in "light" music), its sphere of influence is considerably smaller.

Varied bellows pressure

A rapid increase of bellows pressure causes, apart from the dynamic effect it has, a microtonal shift of the pitch played. As was mentioned earlier, musicians use this to imply shrutis.

However, the modification in pitch is so minute that the technique is also used to create various different effects in other situations. In these cases, it is used as a disguising technique: a desired sound event that is impossible but indispensable is replaced by a vague and universally applicable "something else", compensating the deficits of the instrument. Because of the similarity of the aural effect, this technique is often employed in connection with vocal techniques where the diaphragm plays a role that goes beyond its usual supporting function (e.g. with *gamaka*). But it is also used to compensate for ornaments that are not aurally related, and also to accentuate passage due to various musical reasons.

One rather rare and innovative application of this technique can be heard in a recording of *raga Shuddh Kalyan* by Pt. Bhimsen Joshi .[24] Joshi has been a prominent advocate of the harmonium in *khyal* in the second half of the twentieth century. In this recording, he employs a student vocalist for melodic support, which may seem antiquated, but which is by no means unusual. Also, there is a harmonium accompanist in addition to the supporting singer. This constellation changes the "duties" of the harmonium player; they are spread on two shoulders. This frees the harmonium player to explore new possibilities in his accompaniment style. In this recording, he does so by using the harmonium as a rhythm instrument that fulfils a musical function comparable to that of the bass in European light music. A comparable musical idiom can also be found in the ubiquitous light accordion music, which, given the fact that both instruments produce sound by means of double-reeds, is perhaps no coincidence. In any case, harmonium accompanist Purushottam Walawalkar further reinforces this effect by a rhythmical and sudden increase of bellows pressure. The inclusion of the harmonium into the *tala* is a new functional context for this technique; in this particular performance, Walawalkar makes changes in bellow pressure on a regular basis, and always in sensitive interaction with the *tabla* accompaniment.[25]

* * *

The techniques that have been described here are a selection from the overall range of options at the disposal of a harmonium player when he wants to compensate the shortcomings of his instrument. Naturally, not all musicians use all strategies in the same manner and frequency, nor within the same musical contexts: the personal style of an accompanist is prominently characterised by the tendency to apply one method rather than the other. The stylistic spectrum among musicians is particularly broad when it comes to chords: while some musicians tend to avoid them wherever possible, others use them intensively – for various musical purposes.[26]

In the light of these stylistic divergences, the central question is: what is the function of the accompanying instrument? If it were to imitate the solo voice in as much detail as possible, the harmonium was far from qualifying as suitable. In particular, when compared to the *sarangi*, the harmonium simply fails to live up to this postulation. And yet, musical practice affirms the harmonium's suitability by accepting it as sufficient for its duties. This is how most of the musicians I spoke with put it: the harmonium "suffices", in spite of all its accepted imperfections and drawbacks. This implies that there is a rather flexible bandwidth as far as the accompaniment is concerned, which corresponds to the same phenomenon regarding intonation

This is a conclusion which seems self-sufficient, at first glance, if it were not to be assumed that the willingness and ability to adapt to a given situation is a recent development. For this reason it is subject to harsh criticism, which is not surprising in a culture that attributes much value to the validating force of longevity, particularly in the realm of aesthetics. However, I doubt that this development is related only to the emergence of the harmonium. For during the long decline of Mogul court culture in India, the education of the *sarangi* players – back then the only serious alternative to fill the still new position of the melodic accompanist – suffered, and the music system had to make up for this. Moreover, studying the instrument requires a keen ear. This means that studying the *sarangi* has the prospect of success only if the student brings an above-average talent to the instrument. As social change began, such a musician found open doors to a solo career much more easily if he took on an instrument that was free of social stigmata such as that borne by the *sarangi*. The result of this situation was a chronic shortage of competent *sarangi* players willing to provide accompaniment, which is, time and again, put forward as an argument in favour of the harmonium.[27] Those of my interlocutors who use a harmonium themselves or who advocate its use have pointed out that a badly played *sarangi* is a musical disaster, while using a harmonium ensured a certain degree of quality in a performance: "With the harmonium, it may not be perfect, but at least you are on the safe side: you know the pitch the harmonium player is going to produce, whereas with a *sarangiya*, it is a matter of *gharana*, musical ear and personality."[28] For these singers, the stability in intonation is a main argument for the harmonium. However, there is also another aspect that looms in Hemang Meta's formulation of "personality": a *sarangiya*, common opinion holds, is more self-confident and self-conscious than a harmonium player, and sometimes he even might try to seriously compete with the soloist; "he might just take over and think it is his solo performance."[29] According to my interlocutors, rivalry conflicts between singer and *sarangi* players are by far more frequent than between harmonium player and singer.

From the musical perspective, then, choosing the harmonium over the *sarangi* may be a decision for the "lesser evil". The soloist prefers a relatively inflexible, somewhat inaccurate, yet reliable, intonation, as well as several detriments in terms of musical self-containedness, over an accurate, but potentially inconsistent or undesired, intonation, an otherwise unachievable similarity in timbre to the human voice, and possible communication problems. The decisions for both accompanying instruments that are commonly used nowadays, as well as for a supporting singer, bring along both musical advantages and disadvantages. The determining factor for the statistically evident preference for the harmonium over the *sarangi* is probably the historical development of the profession of the *sarangiya*, with all its musical consequences. However, the harmonium has by no means supplanted the *sarangi*; two processes that started independently from each other – the arrival of the harmonium in India and the changing of the role of the *sarangi* – developed parallel in the late nineteenth and early twentieth centuries.

That, however, the harmonium of all available instruments took over the role of the most popular accompanying instrument is, in my view, due to two general aspects of the instrument and its use. The first one is purely musical in nature: the specific free-reed timbre of the harmonium (see chapter III.1.2). The other one is of sociological interest and relates to the peculiarities of the relationship between vocal soloist and harmonium accompanist in Indian music.

IV.2.2 The Relationship Between Vocal Soloist And Harmonium Accompanist

When compared with richness of nuance, the subtle inflections and the timbral flexibility of the human voice, the harmoniums falls short, which creates a sharp contrast between soloist and accompanist. This, once more, underlines the predominance of the singing voice, much more than would be the case with an accompanying instrument that was able to 'compete' in all three aspects. Emphasising a musical, yet primarily extra-musical, hierarchical relationship is of central importance, and the need for it evolved throughout history, as shall be shown below. The contemporary relationship between vocal soloist and harmonium accompanist was significantly influenced by the historical developments that were described earlier.

The following remarks relate to a somewhat idealised interrelation between musicians. "I am the boss – his role [i.e. the role of the harmonium player] is subordinate"[30]; "Where there is a director general – that is me – then there is an assistant director general [i.e. the harmonium player]..."[31]. Like this or similarly, singers describe their relationship to their harmonium accompanists; none of the musicians whom I spoke to regarded the accompanying function to be on equal footing with the solistic function.

This primacy of the soloist is anchored in the fundamentals of the North Indian music system: the soloist holds the central position. The vocal soloist, moreover, takes the first position among all soloists because the human voice is considered the sound medium that is most flexible of all and that possesses the greatest capabilities. Singing is considered the purest form for the realisation of Indian music.

Of all members of an ensemble, only the singer-soloist is "entitled" to establish the musical flow in a creative manner; the accompanist, on the other hand, is expected to shadow the singer. He is supposed to improvise, but his improvisations are required to remain close to the singer's example. While this "shadowing" includes the realisation of musical ideas to some extent, it is of central importance that the harmonium player contributes to the mood that the singer establishes in the first place.

> He has to continue the design, see what my concept would be. Not doing something which is very contradictory to the design I have started. What I would say, singing is a creative field, and the accompanying artist is working in the creative field. He has to see my creation and support it. Even if I stop and give him space, he has to come to my vision. He has to see it from the singer's point of view. At that time he has to forget that he can also play solo.[32]

The last sentence of this quotation clarifies the position of the accompanist: he has to abandon his own musical conception of how the raga is to be performed, and avoid taking an autonomous effect on it. Rather, the accompanist is supposed to work on the basis of the musical motives provided by the singer and is not supposed to propose his or her own ideas to any significant extent. Since *sangat* requires the accompanist to anticipate the upcoming musical development and, in places, to execute it simultaneously with the soloist, this necessitates a great deal of familiarity between the two musicians, as well as a high amount of musical knowledge and sensibility on the side of the accompanist.

If, then, equally much is demanded from soloist and accompanist, the prestige given the two functions differs greatly. Accompanists are not necessarily considered to be artists who contribute to the *raga* realisation,[33] because only the singer is regarded as the one bringing to the performance the musical genius that makes it successful. Harmonium accompanists are usually trained singers, and in view of the blatant prestige disparity between singer and harmonium player, in spite of their often equally profound musical education, John Napier provocatively asks: "Are melodic accompanists failed soloists?"[34] He concludes that this may indeed sometimes apply to those accompanists whose voices stopped fulfilling professional standards once they had reached adulthood. For them, Napier suggests, a reasonable choice was to pick up the accompanying instrument, whereas a complete transition to a solo instrument is also possible and the harmonium is not the only alternative.

It is a commonly held view that there are many harmonium players because the instrument is so easy to learn, and does not require an intensive study of music. This statement may not be tenable, but it remains very popular.[35] At the bottom of this is the conviction that in order to fulfil his responsibilities, a harmonium player needs less musical competence than a singer. In an exaggerated formulation, the commonly held view of the harmonium player is that of a "second-class" musician.[36] This is a key point: a precondition for qualifying as accompanist is one's willingness to subordinate oneself. This hierarchical component also limits the choice of the accompanying instrument on the part of the singer:

> Players are soloists in Hindustani music. They don't want to accompany. The harmonium is the only thing that is there. You don't take *sitar* or *sarod*, they are solo instruments. Maybe it is a matter of hierarchy. You wouldn't ask a *sitar* player to sit down and accompany you. They are soloists in their own right. Harmonium is not a solo instrument.[37]

A harmonium player has to be conscious of his subordinate position: "I do not try to show more skill than the singer. Sometimes, I have more skills or more thoughts, but then I have to control myself. I have to play within the limits of the singer as well [as within those of] my instrument."[38]

In looking at the array of potential accompanying instruments, it becomes clear that no other instrument is associated with such a clearly subordinate hierarchical position. Ever since the change in the position of the *sarangi* within the social system, the players of which advanced from nameless accompanists to highly respected soloists in their own right, there has been no instrument that aspired to fill the gap that the *sarangi* left during its upward move – none but the harmonium. Earlier circumstances (the *kotha* milieu in particular) have changed, and they have been replaced with other structures, but the hierarchical thinking of the time is similar to the one prevalent in contemporary India. The harmonium is the only instrument that inevitably has to subordinate, because it is contestable.

Yet one group of musicians holds a different view: those who upon the question of why they took up the harmonium would unambiguously and precisely assert that "I just liked the sound of the instrument."[39] For these musicians, professionalizing their harmonium playing is not a lesser evil, but a conscious decision. Such a decision is, in my view, not least based on the notion that a 'subordinate' musician is open to many more professional opportunities than a soloist: apart from accompaniment, he can also work in the profitable field of light music, or be involved in making stage music for local theatre traditions. The occupational profile of a harmonium player sometimes resembles that of a service provider in the creative field of music.

There remains the question of whether a harmonium accompanist contributes to the *raga* realisation, or not. In the perception of the average listener, this question is of little significance; the centre of attention is the soloist, and the rhythmic and the melodic accompanists draw interest only to a much lesser extent. The accompanist, in this view, is an appendage, fulfilling other functions than *raga* realisation: he fills gaps with musical motives that do not advance the musical development, but simply maintain the melodic flow and therefore keep the musical progress in the status quo, anticipating the soloist's return.[40] Most interestingly, in order to perpetuate the 'image' of the *raga* (a formulation that corresponds to the Indian *raga* notion), there is no need for a detailed copy of the (singer's) template; rather a rough sketch is sufficient: "[Being a singer,] I am engrossed in my own ideas. Give me this much [i.e. an indication of the individual notion of the respective *raga*], that plants the idea into my head."[41] This 'frugality' is a rather recent development. The decision for an ideational, rather than a direct, inspiration through the accompanist is a consequence of the choice of the 'safer' way:

the central argument that singer level against *sarangiyas* as accompanists is that there is always the danger that the respective musician – and almost all *sarangi* players perform as soloists today – might not control himself and therefore transgress the limits of his function by actively shaping the *raga* flow and rivalling the singer.[42] With the harmonium, this danger is just not present, first and foremost because of the instrument's technical drawbacks; moreover, harmonium players are accompanists in the first place, and if they are also soloists, solo performances add up to only a small fraction of their overall work. Here, therefore, the danger is practically avoided at the outset because harmonium players do not break these unwritten rules: "I was never hurt by a harmonium player."[43]

Endnotes

1. See Napier, *Sangat* (see note 2).
2. Appa Jalgaonkar, conversation on 7 April 2003.
3. Manohar Chimote and Jitendra Gore consider just intonation capable of realising every *raga*. Therefore they claim to be able to perform any *raga* on a harmonium with just intonation, regardless of the individual *raga's* characteristics. Manohar Chimote and Jitendra Gore, conversation on 9 April 2003.
4. Shruti Sadolikar, *raga* Maru Bihag. Excerpt from the recording published by Joep Bor, Suvarnalata Rao, Wim van der Meer & Jane Harvey in *The Raga Guide. A Survey of 74 Hindustani Ragas*, Monmouth 1999. CD no. 3, track 12. Also see the transcriptions of this recording given by Joep Bor and Henri Tournier.
5. Arawind Thatte, *raga Maru Bihag*. Excerpt from the recording *Harmonium Solo by Dr. Arawind Thatte. Raag Maru Bihag, Sampurna Malakauns & Malakauns*, MC Alurkar Audio Video Products AA 226 Stereo.
6. In the early stage of an *alap*, a *raga*'s tonal material develops without clear-cut rhythmic patterns. Whether an *alaap* is based on regular rhythmic pulse or not remains a debatable question among musicians.
7. Alurkar Audio Video Production, MC AA 226.

8. In Bor et. al., *Raga Guide* (see note 232), p. 112 et seq.
9. Conversations with Shubhangi Bahulikar, 5 April 2003, and Sunita Dhar, 28 April 2003.
10. Arawind Thatte, conversation on 5 April 2003.
11. Arawind Thatte, conversation on 5 April 2003.
12. I encountered two exceptions to this. Manohar Chimote and Jitendra Gore (teacher and student) consider their instruments, which are modified versions of the harmonium that they call *samvadini*, capable of producing the ornaments in question. For further information on the *samvadini*, see Birgit Abels, *The Samvadini – A harmonium more Indian than the Indian harmonium?*, in: *Hefte des Arbeitskreises Harmonium in der GdO* 5 (2003), pp. 26–32.
13. Arawind Thatte, conversation on 5 April 2003.
14. Napier [*Sangat:* (see note 2), pp. 124 et seq.] presents figures that document the growing predominance of the harmonium as accompanying instrument in course of the latter part of the twentieth century.
15. This is examined in depth by Napier, *Sangat* (see note 2).
16. Veena Sahasrabuddhe, conversation on 7 April 2003.
17. Ashok D. Ranade, *Hindustani Music*, Delhi [2]2002, p.137 et seq.
18. Lakshman Krishnarao Pandit (vocals), Dhruba Ghosh (*sarangi*), and Anant Rane (harmonium), *raga Puriya*, track 1, CD 3, of Napier, *Sangat* (see note 2). This music example is a modified version of that found in Napier, *Sangat* (see note 2).
19. Vijay Kichlu (voice). Jyoti Goho (harmonium), *raga Bhairav*, track 3, CD 1, of of Napier, *Sangat* (see note 2). This transcription is a modified version of that found in Napier, *Sangat* (see note 2), p. 522.
20. van der Meer, *Hindustani Music* (see note 213), p. 39.
21. See van der Meer, *Hindustani Music* (see note 213), p. 38 et seq.
22. Arawind Thatte, conversation on 5 April 2003; Jitendra Gore, 9 April 2003; Veena Sahasrabuddhe, 7 April 2003.
23. Modified version of the transcription in Napier, *Sangat* (see note 2), vol. II, p. 344. In the example, harmonium player Arawind Thatte accompanies singer Malini Rajurkar; this is a *khyal* recording.
24. Bhimsen Joshi (vocals), Purushottam Walawalkar (harmonium), *Raga Shuddh Kalyan*, CD *Pandit Bhmsen Joshi in Celebration vol. 3*, navras NRCD 0075.
25. Naturally, the harmonium comes through more clearly manner in those places where bellows pressure is increased abruptly. However, in the recording by Joshi/Walawalkar, the contrast between average and increased bellows pressure is probably greater than originally intended,

probably because of an unfavourable position of the microphones, which amplifies the bass disproportionately more than the higher registers.

26. One musician who dismisses the use of chords is Arawand Thatte. He considers chords as generally alien to the Indian musical system, and confines himself to the absolutely necessary (conversation on 5 April 003). Harmonium accompanist Jyoti Goho, on the other hand, makes ample use of both clusters and chords. Compare the transcription of the raga Bhairav recording with Vijay Kichlu in Napier, *Sangat* (see note 2), vol. II, p. 517 et seq.
27. Veena Sahasrabuddhe, conversation on 7 April 2003; Patanjali Maduskar, 8 April 2003; Hemang Mehta, 8 April 2003; Vikas Kashalkar, 4 April 2003.
28. Hemang Mehta, conversation on 8 April 2003.
29. Veena Sahasrabuddhe, conversation on 7 April 2003.
30. Vikas Kashalkar, conversation on 4 April 2003.
31. Sanjeev Abhyankar, conversation on 3 April 2003.
32. Sanjeev Abhyankar, conversation on 3 April 2003.
33. This is very evident in press reviews, most of which either do not mention the accompanist at all or do not pay much regard to him. Only in rare cases, s/he receives appreciation of his or her musical accomplishment or contribution to the performance.
34. Napier, *Sangat* (see note 2), p. 134.
35. Patanjali Maduskar, conversation on 8 April 2003.
36. Also see Napier, *Sangat* (see note 2), p. 132.
37. Hemang Meta, conversation on 8 April 2003.
38. Arawind Thatte, conversation on 29 September 2003.
39. Arawind Thatte, conversation on 5 April 2003; Appa Jalgaonkar, 7 April 2003.
40. On the necessity, function, and role of the "musical flow," see, for instance, Stephen Slawek, *Keeping it going: Terms, Practices, and Processes of Improvisation in Hindustani Instrumental Music*, in: Bruno Nettl & Melinda Russell (eds.), *In the Course of Performance. Studies in the World of Musical Improvisation*, Chicago & London, 1998, pp. 335–368, particularly p. 336.
41. Vikas Kashalkar, conversation on 4 April 2003 in Pune. Similar thoughts are proposed by Bh. Pingle in the 1890s (*Indian Music*, p. 200).
42. Sanjeev Abhyankar, conversation on 3 April 2003; Veena Sahasrabuddhe, 7 April 2003; Hemang Mehta, 8 April 2003; Wasifuddin Dagar, 28 April 2003.
43. Sanjeev Abhyankar, conversation on 3 April 2003.

V

The Future

In the early days after its introduction to India the harmonium established itself in the British households, as has been seen, in the early stages representing a certain prestige – a remarkable aspect from a current perspective, seeing that the harmonium is anything but a generally prized instrument in Europe today. This prestige factor is also what qualified the harmonium to be preferred above other instruments that by all means had the musical potential to compete with the harmonium – an instrument that especially deserves mention here is the accordion, which spread rapidly at the same time in other parts of the world (albeit in an entirely different context).

The accordion was known early in India, and was used early e.g. in the context of proselytisation.[1] But it came as a "sailor's instrument", and because it failed to shed its image of an instrument for "light" music, it never gained entry to the classical genres of northern India. To this day it is used gladly, but only in "light" music and here especially in fusion or film music.

The concertina had a different "class stigma" than the accordion from the onset: it came from 'cultivated' genres and therefore had a starting position at least fundamentally similar to that of the harmonium. Because no documents could be found it is assumed that the import of concertinas increased at a very slow rate only, for reasons which still are not clear. But independently from that, another aspect might have made the harmonium more attractive for Indian purposes than the concertina and other instruments with button or pin keyboards: the claviature. This genuinely European invention probably increased the preference for the harmonium, and this perhaps not only for the mentioned reasons of prestige, but because of the intuitively comprehensible compatibility between the Indian concept of tonal space and the concept of twelve steps in an octave that are quasi suggested and presented to the musician. Apart from that, the keyboard's concept corresponds to the notation of Indian music, the 12-step *sargam* notation. The keyboard's introduction coincides with the eminent increase of importance of the *sargam*-system in connection with the *raga* classifying system of Pt. V.N. Bhatkhande. It seems likely that the keyboard radiated a certain haptic familiarity that was – apart from volume and timbre – an important factor leading to the seemingly unconditional acceptance of the harmonium.

The question of competition between the harmonium and harmonica-instruments is also relevant in other respects, because there were harmonica-instruments in India, and these seem to have been used in the missionary context.[2] If missionaries report that the accordion as taken along "auf Zeltreisen ins weite Stationsgebiet", "um durch allerlei schöne Weisen die braunen Heiden herbeizulocken",[3] yet hardly mention the harmonium, then these instruments must have had a considerable sphere of influence. Yet they never were accepted, arguably because of the reasons outlined earlier.

What is more important, though, is that this supports the thesis that the harmonium was spread through "cultivated domestic music" and not in the proselytisation process. If the missionaries (coming from several nations, dominated by Germans and largely Protestant) mostly used harmonica-instruments, then this group was not primarily responsible for propagating the harmonium, but only played a subordinate role.

The instrument rapidly gained access to Indian homes, at first in families oriented towards Europe, where it was used for music training and for the performance of European art music, especially palm court music. It was used increasingly in the performance of a distinct form of "cultivated" folk song (especially in Bengal), and after having gained access to Indian music this way it continued to be spread in this initially well-defined area: it "conquered" those Indian households whose affluence was due to trade with the British and which were culturally inclined towards Europe.

But this process not only took place in Bengal, the region which was focussed on in this study because of its abundance of sources: identical processes happened in all the colonial centres in northern India (among others Bombay). It can be assumed that the same happened in southern India; here the process originated not only in British settlements, but also those controlled by the Portuguese and, of even more relevance to the harmonium, French (among others Goa, Pondicherry, Madras). The starting points were urban, but the actual spread took place in rural areas: roaming theatre troupes in particular popularised the instrument, and the harmonium entered the classical genres through those genres performed onstage.

In this early phase most harmoniums were European pedal models. That instruments related to the harmonium (e.g. the harmoniflûte) were present can be verified, and it can be assumed that these instruments were used parallel to the harmonium.

The rapid spread of the harmonium in this form as well as in its later, so-called Indian form was aided by the social changes of the time, which caused a complete restructuring of the music scene in Northern India. The collapse of the Mogul empire and its patronage of the music caused classical music to be 'popularised' in the actual sense and to become publicly accessible and therefore common cultural property.

Another factor not to be underestimated is the origin of distinct genres like *thumri* in the performance of music by courtesans: the *sarangi* acquired the stigma of the indecent and the obscene, something that player and instrument never managed to free themselves of. For this reason an alternative accompanying instrument was looked for, and the harmonium offered obvious advantages: as free reed instrument it could produce a constant sound; its timbre was very close to that of the human voice, and it was considerably louder than the *sarangi*, which accommodated the new performance situation; and finally it was always in tune – not always exactly according to the singers ideals, but still within limits that seemed acceptable.

These circumstances were supported by the changes that took place in the traditionally very strictly hierarchical organisation of Indian music. Within certain limits the harmonium levelled the differences between soloists, differences that then played a role for the first time; for at this time harmonium players never aspired to solo careers, but were subordinate musicians from the outset. This offered an acceptable way out of the dilemma created by the dissolution of the traditional "musicians" castes'.

The harmonium was accepted for various reasons that were not all of musical nature, but during the late 19th and early 20th centuries opposition mounted, rejecting the harmonium and arguing mainly from a theoretical perspective.

The part of the ensuing discussion that can be reconstructed today is limited to written sources. It has been shown that the authors' expressed conception of the nature of Indian music and the resulting demands were based upon ancient sources which are difficult to interpret, or upon the same sources blended with a European sense of mission. The exclusive recourse to sources as well as the idiosyncratic European notion of culture involved here can only be understood in its context: in one case it is about Indian cultural self-image seeing itself between the two poles of its own cultural heritage and the European concept of progress when the colonial period commences; in the other case the new field of Oriental studies, in conjunction with comparative linguistics, discovered a historico-cultural kinship between the two cultures, which led to a retrogressive academic interest in reconstructing a – partially fictitious – past. In this context the cultural, or more concretely: musical present became a secondary object of examination only. Yet this doubtlessly ethnocentric view resulted not from political considerations, but exclusively from an academic fascination which was a product of the time.

An examination of the discussion yields the realisation that the thesis about the harmonium being forced upon the Indians is untenable. If something was forced upon the Indians, then it was the *shruti*-harmonium; the majority of the Europeans who were interested were amazed by the Indians' use of the harmonium, and tried to offer alternatives for this in their opinion "wrong" instrument – alternatives, however, that were not accepted, as was the case with the *shruti*-harmonium.

The currently strongest argument against the harmonium is the tuning, which is unsuitable because it is not flexible. Musicology still has to deal with the topic of intonation in Indian music thoroughly, but studies conducted so far have already shown clearly why Indians are able to use the harmonium in spite of the fact that it can only play 12 fixed pitches per octave.

Mark Levy has shown that in spite of theoretical quantifications North Indian music displays a remarkable flexibility as far as intonation is concerned. A close look at Levy's results shows clearly that with regards to the singing voice, tempered tuning is also normal: if this conceded flexibility is transferred to the harmonium, neither the use of an inflexible scale nor its division of the octave into twelve steps should be a problem. Yet this is one of the central arguments against the harmonium's use. This obvious contradiction between the prevalent practice and argumentative logic suggests that something else is the driving force behind the argument of the harmonium's incorrect tuning.

This "something else" is disproportionately complicated and is not limited entirely to the intonation's flexibility (as with the human voice and all the instruments used in Indian music, to a certain degree also the "imported" *santur*).

An examination of the relationship between singer and accompanist has shown that the singer leads and that the accompanist has to follow (even to the point of repeating mistakes[4]. This seems to be at the core of the conflict: if a scale is fixed, it is solely the singer's responsibility to define how this scale is fixed. This thesis, that it is less about parameters imminent to the music but much more about external factors, is supported by the fact that what is regarded as the harmonium's worst shortcoming – the fixed, in the "worst" case tempered tuning – is also present in the singing in a very similar form, but this is either not realised or just not mentioned.[5] This negation regarding the vocalist shows that, when compared to the same fact regarding the harmonium, the criticism of the harmonium is less about reality than about pretence: A harmonium can never satisfy the demands of North Indian music theory, but a singer can; if he also does is an entirely different question.

For many Indians, the necessity to have a closer look at this is not the consequent desideratum it seems to be for Europeans. Vikas Kashalkar's statement cited earlier is very revealing: "Give me this much, that plants the idea into my head."[6] This ultimately means that the perception of music in India has a completely different nature than in Europe, in fact much more than has been allowed for in the literature until now. The individual listener has an ideal conception of a certain *raga* and hears it inwardly – the actual, simultaneously performed *raga* rather is a means of putting this inward process into motion. Also in the further course of the performance the real sound influences the individual perception of the music insofar as it does not oppose hearing the ideal inwardly, or that it (in the worst case) makes it impossible. The shades between the two extremes are defined by how many points of contact with his ideal concept the musician can give the listener. This pertains to concepts of music; in the same manner it deals with the emotional content of each *raga*, whereas not the *raga*'s absolute interpretation plays a role, but its effect on the listener: "Each *raga* is to be performed with this aspect [of a certain emotional mood] in mind, so that the appropriate mood can be evoked in the listener's mind."[7]

According to the traditional opinion this emotional effect can only be possible when the *raga* is performed correctly. According to many well-known legends, the effects that *ragas* are said to have approach the mystical to some extent. The legendary singer of Akbar's times, Tansen, one day performed the *raga Dipak*, of which it is said that it can light lamps or set the singer ablaze if performed correctly. Tansen was close to bursting into flames when his wife realised the danger and sang the *raga Miyan Mallar,* which can let it rain.[8] The contemporary first interpretation of such legends would be to consider these myths in a metaphorical sense and to see the fire for a distinct, strong emotion, and the same with the rain. This approach is not shared by a large number of classically trained Indian musicians: to some extent they understand the legends literally. The fact that the described consequences – e.g. a singer going up in flames – do not occur is explained with reference to the decline of musical abilities, also those of professional musicians.[9] Such an argument is based on the assumption that today's music culture is only a shadow of what it used to be (which corresponds with the concept of tradition mentioned earlier, in which making music today is inevitably linked with the past) – here, too, it is tacitly assumed that there is an ideal that is known to musicians and which they aspire to, but will not be able to reach (any more).

The relationship between musical ideal and musical reality in India and its culmination in a way of listening that is fixated on an ideal is obviously a highly complex topic that still needs investigation. What is described above is the perception of many Indian musicians as well as traditional musicologists. This group comprises the largest part of the active classical musicians, i.e. the group that widely uses the harmonium and therefore "creates" culture. In addition, a very high level of music education is expected from the audience – perhaps this explains why the Indian literature time and again and in various contexts refers to the Indian audience's above-average musical competence and power of judgement.

In the context of the harmonium's use it can be noted that at the root of the discussion, whether the harmonium is suitable for Indian music or not, there is the relation of claim and reality. While the harmonium by all means offers an acceptable solution for musicians, an argumentation influenced in part by an academic standpoint based on a European perspective cannot agree with the outlined notion of an "unreachable ideal".

Different conceptions of tradition clash, as I showed in Chapter II.2. Those who reject the harmonium are a small group of people arguing mainly academically, whereas those who propagate the instrument are mostly active musicians. These two groups simply do not speak the same language: the musicians use the medium of their music, mostly without explaining their actions verbally; the others make much less music, but mainly use the discursive channels of written language.

This constellation started developing from the onset of the harmonium's presence in India. In the colonial context the "case" of the harmonium shows that between the coloniser and the colonised there seems to be a kind of "neutral sphere" in which colonial theories are secondary, if not irrelevant: in music. But what is to be clearly differentiated from that is the discussion itself, because this is where the supposedly clear border between colonial power and the colonised does not apply. The hegemonic structures do not become meaningless, on the contrary: they especially foster the somewhat elitist adoption of European thought by some Indians.

Another complex which influences the phenomenon of the harmonium in Indian music is the relationship between transition processes in music and the Indian conception of tradition. The necessity to ground everyday practice on a reference to an authoritative, ancient tradition – Hobsbawm's idea of an "invented tradition"[10] inevitably comes to mind – was not only seen by the musicians and musicologists I interviewed; musicological texts also often make references of this kind, without expounding how these relationships were arrived at and without providing evidence.[11]

In this light it is obvious that the colonial situation fostered this phenomenon. This complex is very interesting with regard to India and an investigation of the conception of tradition and its mutual influence on modern music certainly would yield revealing insights into the mechanisms of interaction between tradition and change. For our purposes it would suffice to note that, with reference to the harmonium, North Indian classical music is not the archival vacuum it has often been described as, and still is by some to this day. The classic and often cited model of the Great Tradition[12] does no justice to reality, because it ignores any organic development which renews and changes culture constantly, even if these processes do not leave clear evidence.

This study has shown clearly that the harmonium is seen by most of its advocates as a compromise. Also the most prevalent, largely feasible adaptation of the instrument to Indian requirements – tuning the instrument to individual needs – can and should not mean that the instrument has been perfected. The question poses itself whether it is not precisely this little imperfection that is needed in the accompanying role: if the harmonium is limited to being an accompanying instrument, also because the strict hierarchy limits the possibilities of the accompanist, it extends the freedom of the singer – a desideratum that only emerged with the musico-social changes described in Chapter II.1.1.

So can a harmonium player perform a *raga* or not? To date this question has not been answered by current musical practice. It is also not as decisive as it seems; if the harmonium is used as an accompanying instrument, it is not really necessary: it acts as a filler that should not introduce its own musically creative ideas, because that would mean competition for the singer and his privileges. It suffices when the singer uses the strategies described in Chapter IV.2.1 to minimize the deficiencies – it plays the role of a musically subordinate instrument whose function it is not to use the full spectrum of musical expression, but to provide melodic accompaniment.

For this the question need not be answered, for it does not pose itself. It is not in the accompanying context that practice might find an answer at all, but in the context of using the harmonium as a solistic instrument. Here it will be decided whether the harmonium will after all establish itself as a fully-fledged instrument in Indian music or not – a decision solely in the hands of the musicians and music aficionados, as was the case with the harmonium as an accompanying instrument.

Endnotes

1. See Christoph Wagner, *Zur Rezeption und weltweiten Verbreitung der Handharmonikainstrumente*, in: Monika Lustig (ed.), *Harmonium und Handharmonika*, Blankenburg 2002, pp. 195–202.
2. See the corresponding quotes and graphic material by Wagner, *Handharmonikainstrumente* (see note 272), p. 198 et seq.
3. Hohner-Klänge (1930 [1929?]), p. 33, cited in Wagner, *Handharmonikainstrumente* (see note 272), p. 198.
4. See Napier, *Sangat* (see note 2), p. 210 et seq.
5. To what extent the measurements made by Levy and others deviate from older habits cannot be substantiated for lack of data; it can be assumed, however, that especially the intonation was subject to greater variation than today, because recordings influence musicians' education.
6. Vikas Kashalkar, conversation on 4 April 2003 in Pune.
7. Sandeep Bagchee, *Nad. Understanding Raga Music*, Mumbai 1998, p. 82.
8. These legends are scattered over the Indian music literature, with varying intentions. Among others also in Sandeep Bagchee, *Nad. Understanding Raga Music*, Mumbai 1998, p. 82 et seq.
9. This argument was put forward by Sunita Dhar, Professor for sitar at the University of Delhi. Conversation on 30 April 2003.
10. Eric Hobsbawm, *Introduction: Inventing Traditions*, in: Eric Hobsbawm Terence Ranger (eds.), *The Invention of Tradition*, Cambridge et al. 1983, pp. 1–14.
11. Reference to ancient tradition or to prominent persons who are said to have endorsed the argumentation are often presented as final and conclusive. E.g. the musicologist B.C. Deva argues that free reeds were an Indian invention: "in other words the beginning of the harmonium

is in our country." [Bigamudre Chaitanyu Deva, *The Harmonium and Indian Music*, in: *Journal of the Indian Musicological Society* 12/3–4 (September/December 1981), pp. 45–52, here p. 45.]. Only through this statement does he justify the practice of the "great Ustads".

12. Singer, *Great Tradition* (see note 119).

Appendix

Measurements

Some of the frequency analyses presented here were conducted with Jonas Braasch, Rensselaer Polytechnic Institute Troy, New York (USA).

Measurement 1

Harmonium of the company Dwarkin & Son Ltd., Kolkata; a = 348 Hz.

Lower octave												
	C	C#	D	D#	E	F	F#	G	G#	A	B@	B
Frequency (Hz)	104	110	117	124	131	139	147	155	165	174	185	196
Cent	0	108	205	305	406	505	607	701	805	903	1006	1107
Abs. distance from the previous pitch		108	97	100	101	99	102	94	104	97	103	101
Cent lower quartile	-3	107	203	303	405	504	606	700	804	902	1005	1106
Cent upper quartile	1	109	207	307	407	505	609	702	805	903	1007	1107
Error 1	4170	1401	2400	2698	2997	2252	1601	2301	2501	2301	1770	2027
Error 2	1	1	1	0.899	0.999	0.979	1	1	1	1	0.885	0.845

Middle octave												
	C	C#	D	D#	E	F	F#	G	G#	A	B@	B
Frequency (Hz)	207	220	233	246	261	276	293	310	329	348	369	392
Cent	1199	1305	1401	1501	1603	1698	1803	1900	2002	2099	2201	2305
Abs. distance from the previous pitch	92	106	96	100	102	95	105	97	102	97	102	104
Cent lower quartile	1199	1304	1401	1500	1602	1698	1803	1900	2000	2098	2200	2304
Cent upper quartile	1201	1305	1402	1501	1603	1698	1803	1900	2003	2099	2203	2305
Error 1	1787	2301	1401	1824	2001	2501	2338	1501	1155	2001	2001	1801
Error 2	0.893	1	1	0.912	1	1	0.974	1	0.963	1	1	1

Upper octave				
	C	C#	D	D#
Frequency (Hz)	413	440	464	494
Cent	2396	2504	2596	2704
Abs. deviation from the previous pitch	91	108	92	108
Cent lower quartile	2395	2503	2596	2703
Cent upper quartile	2397	2505	2597	2705
Error 1	821	1699	1070	241
Error 2	0.667	0.999	0.713	0.031

Tab. 1: Measurement results

		maj. second	maj. third	fourth	fifth	maj. sixth	min. seventh	octave
Dwarkin	bottom octave	205	406	505	701	903	1107	1199
	middle octave	202	404	499	701	900	1106	1197
	upper octave	200						
Just intonation		204	408	498	702	906	1110	1200
Average: Dwarkin		203,5	402	502	701	901,5	1106,5	1198
Tempered tuning		200	400	500	700	900	1100	1200

Tab. 2: Comparison of interval sizes: tuning of the examined instrument, just intonation, tempered tuning.

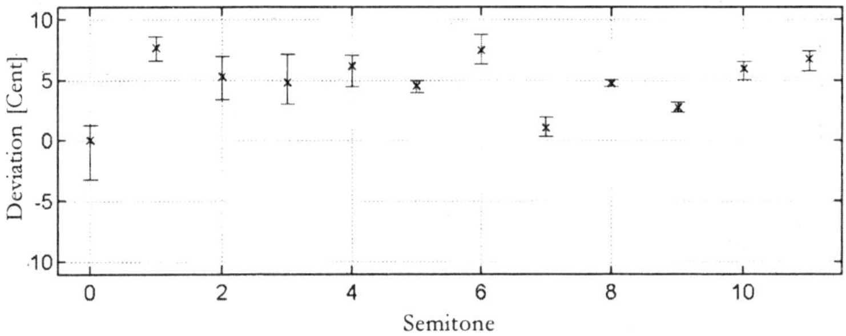

Fig. A.1: Deviation from tempered tuning in the bottom octave of the harmonium made by Dwarkin & Son Ltd. The crosses show the median, the vertical lines upper and lower quartiles.

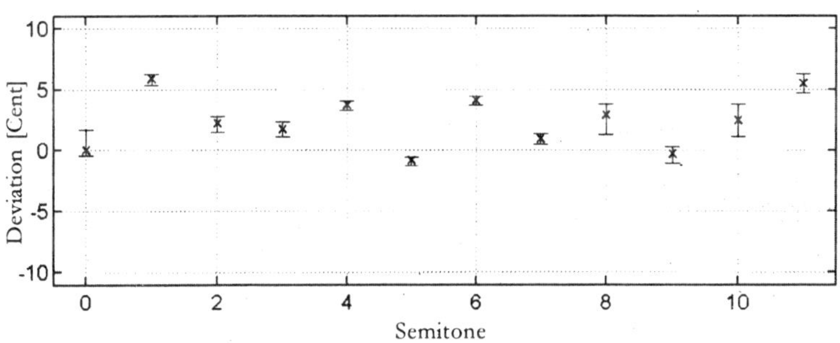

Fig. A.2: Deviation from tempered tuning in the middle octave of the harmonium made by Dwarkin & Son Ltd. The crosses show the median, the vertical lines upper and lower quartiles.

Measurement 2

Instrument of the company Pakrashi & Co., Kolkata; a = 441 Hz.

Lower octave												
	C	C#	D	D#	E	F	F#	G	G#	A	B@	B
Frequency (Hz)	132	139	148	156	165	175	186	197	208	221	234	248
Cent	0	96	198	296	396	493	596	696	795	894	995	1098
Abs. distance from the previous pitch		96	102	98	100	97	103	100	99	99	101	103
Cent lower quartile	-1	95	198	295	394	492	594	696	794	894	994	1098
Cent upper quartile	1	98	199	296	398	494	597	698	797	895	995	1099
Error 1	1025	1504	2053	1799	1750	1670	1459	1704	963	1710	1665	1931
Error 2	1	0.654	0.978	0.899	0.875	0.726	0.663	0.741	0.535	0.743	0.876	0.966

Middle octave												
	C	C#	D	D#	E	F	F#	G	G#	A	B@	B
Frequency (Hz)	262	278	294	312	331	350	371	393	416	441	466	496
Cent	1195	1296	1395	1495	1598	1694	1795	1897	1992	2095	2190	2296
Abs. distance from the previous pitch	97	101	99	100	103	101	101	102	95	103	95	106
Cent lower quartile	1195	1295	1395	1494	1598	1693	1794	1896	1992	2095	2189	2294
Cent upper quartile	1196	1297	1395	1495	1599	1694	1795	1897	1993	2096	2191	2297
Error 1	1935	1659	1701	2301	1804	2001	1701	1865	1901	1416	1943	392
Error 2	0.968	0.79	1	1	0.902	1	1	0.888	1	0.708	0.972	0.196

Upper octave									
	C	C#	D	D#	E	F	F#	G	G#
Frequency (Hz)	524	556	589	622	660	699	742	787	831
Cent	2394	2496	2595	2691	2793	2892	2995	3099	3193
Abs. distance from the previous pitch	98	102	99	96	102	99	103	104	96
Cent lower quartile	2393	2495	2594	2690	2793	2891	2994	3097	3191
Cent upper quartile	2394	2496	2595	2692	2794	2892	2995	3099	3193
Error 1	351	2101	1993	1915	915	552	1655	1368	270
Error 2	0.175	1	0.997	0.958	0.508	0.325	0.871	0.76	0.844

Tab. 3: Measurement results.

		maj. second	maj. third	fourth	fifth	maj. sixth	min. seventh	octave
Pakrashi	bottom octave	198	396	493	696	894	1098	1195
	middle octave	200	403	499	702	900	1101	1199
	upper octave	201	399	498	705			
Just intonation		204	408	498	702	906	1110	1200
Average: Dwarkin		199,67	399,3	496,67	701	897	1099,5	1197
Tempered tuning		200	400	500	700	900	1100	1200

Tab. 4: Comparison of interval sizes: tuning of the examined instrument, just intonation, tempered tuning

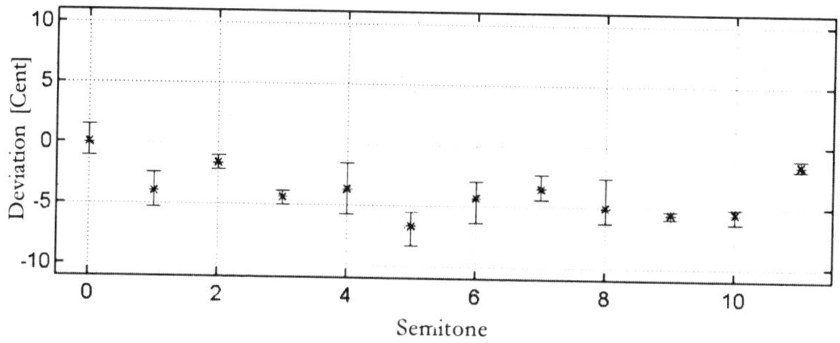

Fig. A.3: Deviation from tempered tuning in the bottom octave of the harmonium made by Pakrashi & Co. The crosses show the median, the vertical lines upper and lower quartiles.

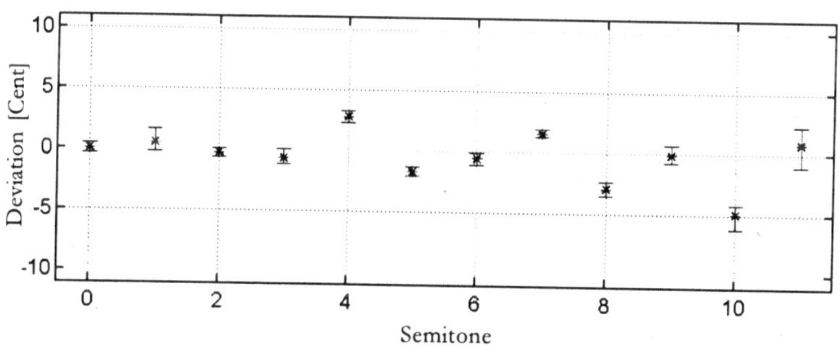

Fig. A.4: Deviation from tempered tuning in the middle octave of the harmonium made by Pakrashi & Co. The crosses show the median, the vertical lines upper and lower quartiles.

This study incorporates information gathered during several research trips to India between 2001 and 2003. Conversations with the following people have influenced this study:

Sanjeev Abhyankar, singer, Pune
Meraj Ahmed, singer (Qawwali), Delhi
Shubhangi Bahulikar, singer and musicologist (University Pune), Pune
Shubha Chaudhury, musicologist, Gurgaon
Manohar Chimote, harmonium- and samvadini player, Thane
Wasifuddin Dagar, singer (Dhrupad), Delhi
Claire Devos, scholar of Oriental studies and concert manager, Delhi
Sunita Dhar, sitar player and director of the Music
Jitendra Gore, harmonium- and samvadini player, Mumbai
Manisha Gore, singer, Mumbai
Pratap Ghosh, harmonium maker, Kolkata
Vijay Jagtap, sitar player, London
Appa Jalgaonkar, harmonium player, Pune
Ulhas Kashalkar, singer, Kolkata
Vikas Kashalkar, singer, Pune
Patanjali Maduskar, deputy director of the All India Radio station Mumbai
Hemang Mehta, singer, Mumbai
Suphal Pakrashi, harmonium maker, Kolkata
Suvoji Pakrashi, harmonium maker, Kolkata
Veena Sahasrabuddhe, singer, Mumbai
Tej Kumar Sharma, music instrument dealer, Ahmedabad
Bhajan Sopori, All India Radio, Delhi
Rekha Surya, singer (Thumri), Delhi
Arawind Thatte, harmonium player, Pune

Glossary

Andolan: Slow, wave-like oscillation on a certain pitch

Alap: *Raga*-exposition without rhythmic accompaniment at the beginning of a performance, and which introduces the tonal material of the *raga*; no rhythmic/structural pattern is discernable.

Brahmo Samaj: Religious, monotheistic movement, which rejects iconolatry and the caste system.

Dhrupad: (1) Classical genre in which *raga* and *tala* are performed most strictly. (2) A composition in the *dhrupad*-style.

Gamaka: (1) General term for ornaments. (2) Specific ornament consisting of an abrupt and virtuoso repetition of two notes.

Gat: Instrumental composition usually lasting two *tala*-rounds and followed by improvisation.

Gharana: (1) Musical "school", teaching tradition. (2) A complex of stylistic characteristics in music.

Jhala: Part of an instrumental performance following *alap* and *jor*, characterised by the rapid repetition of single notes.

Jor: [also: *jod*] Part of an instrumental performance between *alap* and *jhala*; not structured by rhythmic patterns, but the musical pulse is audible.

Kan

Khatka: Ornament playing around a main pitch.

Khyal: [also: *khayal*] predominat classical vocal genre of North Indian music.

Kotha: Courtesan parlour

Mind: [also: *mir*, *mindh, midh*] Slowly executed glissando between two or more notes.

Nawab: (1) Regional vice-ruler in India. (2) An affluent, retired Anglo-Indian.

Raga

Samvadi: Second central scale degree in a *raga.*

Shruti: Microtone

Tala: "time-cycle": a rhythmic pattern which forms the basis of every composition and is repeated cyclically.

Tan

Thumri: Semi-classical genre, differing from the 'more classical' genres in the less strict performance of *raga* and *tala*.

Vadi: Central scale degree in a *raga.*

List of music examples:

Music example 1: Arawind Thatte, raga Maru Bihag. Excerpt from the recording *Harmonium Solo by Dr. Arawind Thatte. Raga Maru Bihag, Sampurna Malakauns & Malakauns*, MC Alurkar Audio Video Products AA 226 Stereo. Transcription: Birgit Abels.

Music example 2: Direct comparison of *gamaka* execution by a *sarangi* (middle system) and harmonium (lowest system). Transcription by John Napier.

Music example 3: Compensation of an *andolan* by means of chords. Harmonium (lower system) and voice (upper system). Transcription by John Napier.

Music example 4: *Mind* imitation by filling the intervalic 'gap'. The vocal part is notated in the upper, the harmonium part in the lower line. Transcription by John Napier.

Bibliography

Abels, Birgit : *Harmoniumbau in Indien*, in: *Hefte des Arbeitskreises Harmonium in der GdO* 4 (2002), pp. 27–33

The Samvadini. A harmonium more Indian than the Indian harmonium?, in: *Hefte des Arbeitskreises Harmonium in der GdO 5* (2003), pp. 26–32

Aggarwal, Vinay K. : *Traditions and Trends in Indian Music*, Meerut 1966

Ahmad, Najma Perveen : *Hindustani Music. A Study of its Development in 17th and 18th Centuries*, Delhi 1984

Ahrens, Christian & Klinke, Gregor (eds.): *Das Harmonium in Deutschland: Bau, wirtschaftliche Bedeutung und musikalische Nutzung eines "historischen" Musikinstrumentes*, Frankfurt a. M. 1996

Ahrens, Christian : *Ein griechischer Volksmusiker und sein Instrument, Zur Stimmung folkloristischer Aerophone*, in: Erich Stockmann (ed.), *Studia Instrumentorum Musicae Popularis* VII, Stockholm 1981, pp. 95–101

Zur Frühgeschichte der Instrumente mit Durchschlag-zungen in Europa, in: Monika Lustig (ed.), *Harmonium und Handharmonika*, Blankenburg 2002, pp. 31–50

Athavale, V.R. : *A Historical Account of Marathi Stage Music*, in: *National Centre for the Performing Arts Quarterly Journal* 7 (June) 1978, pp. 16–29

Atre, Prabha : *Modernity in Khyal: Some Notes*, in: *Sangeet Natak: Journal of the Sangeet Natak Akademi* 89–90 (July–December 1988). Special Issue on Tradition and Modernity, pp. 16–23

Enlightening the listener. Contemporary North Indian Classical Vocal Music Performance, New Delhi 2000

Awasthy, G.C. : *Broadcasting in India*, Bombay et al. 1965

Bagchee, Sandeep : *Nad. Understanding Raga Music*, Mumbai 1998

Banerjea, H.D. : *A Comprehensive Self-Instructor for the Setar, Esrar, Violin, Flute, and Harmonium*, Calcutta 1868

Banerjee, Krishna Dhan : *Gita Sutra Sar* [1886]. Translated from the original Bengali as by Himansu Sekhar Banerji: *Translator's Explantions and Notes to Krishna Dhan Banerjee's Gita Sutra Sar, vol. 2, part 2*, Calcutta 1941

Banerjee, Sumanta : *Bad Days for the Ghazal*, in: *The Times of India*, Bombay 26 December 1976, p. 13

The Parlour and the Streets. Elite and Popular Culture in Nineteenth Century Calcutta, Calcutta 1998

Bhatkhande, V. N. : *Music Systems in India*, Delhi 1984

Bhattacharya, Ram Jeevan : *Sruti-Harmonium and its Usefulness*, in: *Journal of the Sangeet Research Academy* 14 (2000), pp. 21–25

BINA, Company : Company Catalogue, no place [Delhi] no date [after 2000]

Booth, D. Gregory : *Brass Bands: Tradition, Change and the Mass Media in Indian Wedding Music*, in: *Ethnomusicology* 34 (2) (1990), pp. 245–262

Bor, Joep : *The Voice of the Sarangi: An illustrated history of bowing in India*, in: *National Centre for the Performing Arts Quarterly Journal* 15 (3, 4) and 16 (1), pp. 1-183

Bor, Joep & Bruguiere, Philippe : *Masters of Raga*, Berlin 1992

Bor, Joep , Rao; Suvarnalata , Meer, Wim van der , & Harvey, Jane : *The Raga Guide. A Survey of 74 Hindustani Ragas*, Nimbus Records, Monmouth 1999

Bosanquet, R.H.M. : *On the Hindu Division of the Octave*, in: Sourindo Mohun Tagore, *Hindu Music from Various Authors*, Varanasi 1965 [1875], p. 317–335

Braasch, Jonas & Klinke, Gregor : *...That Bane of Indian Music - Das Harmonium in Indien*, in: Monika Lustig (ed.): *Harmonium und Handharmonika. 20. Musikinstrumentenbau-Symposium Michaelstein, 19. bis 21. November 1999*, Blankenburg 2002

Byron, Reginald (ed.): *Music, Culture, & Experience. Selected Papers of John Blacking*, Chicago 1995

Capwell, Charles : *Musical Life in 19th-century Calcutta as a component in the History of a Secondary Urban Center*, in: *Asian Music* 18 (1986), pp. 139-163

Marginality and Musicology in Nineteenth-Century Calcutta: The Case of Sourindro Mohun Tagore, in: Bruno Nettl & Philip V. Bohlman, *Comparative Musicology and Anthropology of Music: Essays on the History of Ethnomusicology*, Chicago 1991

Carthy, Maud Mac : *Indian Musical Education*, in: *Modern Review* June 1911

Chatterjee, Chhaya : *Sastriya Sangita and Music Culture of Bengal through the Ages* vol.1, Delhi 1996

Chaudhuri, Manjusree : *Indian Music in Professional and Academic Institutions*, Delhi 1999

Cheveigné, Alain de & Kawahara, Hideki : *YIN, a fundamental frequency estimator for speech and music*, in: *Journal of the Acoustical Society of America* vol. 111 (2002), p. 1917–1930

Chowdhury, Harendra Kishore Roy : *The Musicians of India (Illustrated), Part I*, Calcutta 1929

Clements, Ernest : *Introduction to the Study of Indian Music*, Allahabad 1912, London 1913

The Ragas of Hindusthan, vol. I & II, Poona 1918 & 1921

Lectures on Indian Music, Bombay 1927

Comettant, Oscar : *La Musique, les musiciens et les instruments de musique. Exposition Universelle de 1867*, Portier, no date

Coomaraswamy, Ananda K. : *The Dance of Shiva*, New Delhi 1976 [[1]1918]

Indian Music and Harmoniums, in: *Dawn Magazine* 8 (2), 1912, pp. 74-77

Cousins, Margaret E. : *The Music of the Orient and the Occident: Essays towards Mutual Understanding*, Madras 1935

The Music of Hindustan, in: Usha Sharma, *Heritage of Indian Music*, Jaipur 1996, vol. 1, pp. 15–24

India's Gift of Song, in: Usha Sharma, *Heritage of Indian Music*, Jaipur 1996, vol. 2, pp. 179–187

Music in India in 1935, in: Usha Sharma, *Heritage of Indian Music*, Jaipur 1996 vol. 1

Dahlhaus, Carl : *Arthur Joachim von Oettingen*, in: *Musik in Geschichte und Gegenwart 1*, Kassel et al. 1957, vol. 9, col. 1891 et seq.

Day, C.R. : *The Music and Musical Instruments of Southern India and the Deccan*, London 1891

Dena, Lal : *Christian Missions and Colonialism. A Study of Missionary Movement in North East India With Particular Reference to Manipur and Lushai Hills 1894–1947*, Shillong 1988 [printed Delhi 1979]

Desai, Vasant Shantaram : *Years of Glory. 1880–1920*, in: *The Marathi Theatre*, Bombay 1963

Deshpande, Vamanrao Hari : *Harmonium as Accompaniment For Hindustani Classical Music*, in: *Journal of the Sangeet Natak Akademi* 20 (1971), pp. 15–19

Aesthetic Laws of Khyal, in: *Journal of the Indian Musicological Society* 3 (4), 1972, pp. 12–18

Between two Tanpuras, Bombay 1989

Deva, Bigamudre Chaitanya : *Tradition and Non-Conformity in Indian Music*, in: *Journal of the Indian Musicological Society*, 6 (4) (1975), pp. 27–30

The harmonium and Indian music, in: *Journal of the Indian musicological society* 12/3-4 (Sep-Dec 1981), pp. 45–52

Dieterlen, Michel : *L'Harmonium*, Villeneuve d'Ascq 1999

Dräger, Hans Heinz : *Paul von Janko*, in: *Musik in Geschichte und Gegenwart 1*, Kassel et al. 1957, vol. 6, col. 1710–1713

Ducuing, Fr. (ed.): *Exposition Universelle de 1867 illustrée. Publication internationale autorisée par la commission impériale*, Paris 1867

Dunkel, Maria : *Bandoneon und Konzertina. Ein Beitrag zur Darstellung des Instrumententypus*, Munich & Salzburg 1987

Dunkel, Maria & Fett, Armin : *Harmonikainstrumente*, in: Ludwig Finscher (ed.), *Musik in Geschichte und Gegenwart 2*, Sachteil vol. 4, Kassel et al. 1996

Dwarkin & Son Ltd.: *Dwarkin made it first in the world – Dwarkin does it best in the world* (advertising material), Kolkata 1997

Ellis, Alexander J. : *On the Musical Scales of Various Nations*, in: *Journal of the Society of the Arts* Nr. 1688, vol. XXXIII (27 March 1885), pp. 485–527

Erdman, Joan : *The Maharaja's Musicians: The Organization of Cultural Performances at Jaipur in the 19th Century*, in: Sylvia Vatuk (ed.), *American Studies in the Anthropology of India*, New Delhi 1978, p. 342 et seq.

Arts Patronage in India. Methods, Motives and Markets, Manohar 1992

Farrell, Gerry : *The Early Days of the Gramophone Industry in India: Historical, Social and Musical Perspectives*, in: *British Journal of Ethnomusicology*, Vol. 2

(1993), pp. 31-53

Indian Music and the West, Oxford 1997

Fransson, Frans, Sundberg; Johan & Tjernlund, Per : *The Scale in Played Music*, in: *Svensk tidskrift för musikforskning* 56:1 (1974), pp. 49–54

Fricke, Jobst P. : *Pitch bending und das Harmonium als Reininstrument. Mit einem Verzeichnis der Reininstrumente und deren Beschreibung*, in: Monika Lustig (ed.), *Harmonium und Handharmonika*, Blankenburg 2002, pp. 105–116

Gautam, M.R. : *Evolution of Râga and Tâla in Indian Music*, Delhi 1989

Ghose, Loke Nath : *The Modern history of the Indian Chiefs, Rajas, Zamindars, &c.: Part II The Native Aristocracy and Gentry*, Calcutta 1881

Ghose, Santidev : *Music and Dance in Rabindranath Tagore's Education Philosophy*, Delhi 1978

Goswami, B.N. : *Broadcasting: The new Patron of Indian Music*, Delhi 1996

Gupta, Nilaksha : *Much ado about nothing. The harmonium controversy*, in: *The Telegraph* 28 April 1989

How Does Music Mean? Embodied Memories and the Politics of Affect in the Indian "sarangi", in: American Ethnologist, Vol. 27, No. 4 (Nov., 2000), pp. 805-838

Hobsbawm, Eric : *Introduction: Inventing Traditions*, in: Eric Hobsbawm and Terence Ranger (eds.), *The Invention of Tradition*, Cambridge et al. 1983, pp. 1–14

Hobsbawm, Eric & Ranger, Terence (eds.): *The Invention of Tradition*, Cambridge et al. 1983

Jahan, Ishrat : *Indian Music And Its Assessment: A Sociological Perspective*, Delhi 2002

Jairazbhoy, Nazir Ali : *Intonation in Present-Day North Indian Classical Music*, *Bulletin of the School of Oriental and African Studies* 26 (1963), pp. 119–132

The Ragas of North Indian Music, London 1971

An interpretation of the Twenty-two Shruti, in: *Asian Music* 6 (1975), pp. 38–59

Sangeet Kala Vihar, English Supplement, vol. 1 [incorporated into] Journal of the Indian Musicological Society, vols. 2–5, 1971–4. R. C. Mehta, ed. Baroda: Jambu bet, Dandia Bazar, in : *Ethnomusicology* 19 (1975), pp. 316–318

James, Lawrence : *Raj. The Making and Unmaking of British India*, New York1997

Jeyaraj, Daniel : *Inkulturation in Tranquebar. Der Beitrag der frühen dänisch-halleschen Mission zum Werden einer indisch-einheimischen Kirche (1706–1730)*, Erlangen 1996

Kasliwal, Suneera : *Classical Musical Instruments*, New Delhi 2001

Keshkar, B.V. : *Indian Music: Problems and Prospects*, Bombay 1967

Kopf, David : *British Orientalism and the Bengali Renaissance: The Dynamics of Indian Modernization 1773–1835*, Berkeley 1969

Kramrisch, Stella : *Artist, Patron and Public in India*, in: *Far Eastern Quarterly* 15 (1956), pp. 335–342

L'Armand, Kathleen & Adrian : *Music in Madras: The Urbanization of a Cultural Tradition*, in: Bruno Nettl (ed.), *Eight Urban Musical Cultures*, Urbana 1978

Laird, M.A. : *Missionaries and Education in Bengal 1793–1837*, Oxford 1972

Lettermoser, Werner : *Hermann von Helmholtz*, in: *Musik in Geschichte und Gegenwart 1*, Kassel et al. 1957, vol. 6, col. 125–127

Levy, Mark : *Intonation in North Indian Music: A Select Comparison of Theories with Contemporary Practice*, New Delhi 1982

Liebau, Heike : *Die Quellen der Dänisch-Halleschen Mission in Tranquebar in deutschen Archiven. Ihre Bedeutung für die Indienforschung*, Berlin 1993

Linden, Bob van der : *Music, Theosophical spirituality, and empire: the British modernist composers Cyril Scott and John Foulds*, Journal of Global History 2008 (3), pp. 163-183

Luthra, H.R. : *Indian Broadcasting*, Delhi 1986

Maitra, Madhumanti : *Harmonium now indispensable*, in: *The Telegraph* 28. April 1989

Manuel, Peter : *The Harmonium in Indian and Indo-Caribbean Music. From Colonial Tool to Nationalist Icon*, in: *Free-Reed Journal* vol. 1 (1999), p. 48–59

Thumri in Historical and Stylistic Perspective, Delhi 1989

Cassette Culture: Popular Music And Technology In North India, Oxford 2001

Massey, Reginald & Jamila : *The Music of India*, Delhi 1976

Mayor, Geeta : *The raaga in the Twentieth Century*, in: *Music East and West* (= report of the conference with the same title in Delhi, February 1964), pp. 151–157

Meer, Wim van der : *Hindustani Music in the 20th Century*, The Hague 1980

Mehta, R.C. (ed.): *Thumri: Tradition and Trend, Indian Musicological Society*, Mumbai & Baroda 1990

Ministry of Information & Broadcasting: *Aspects of Indian Music*, Delhi 1957

Mullick, K.S. : *Tangled Tapes: The Inside Story of Indian Broadcasting*, New Delhi 1974

Napier, John : *The Introduction and Use of the Harmonium in North Indian Classical Music*, M.A. thesis (Ms.): University of New South Wales, Sydney 1994

Sangat: Melodic Accompaniment in North Indian Vocal Music, PhD (Ms.): University of New South Wales, Sydney 2001

An Old Tradition but a Very New Practice: Accompaniment and the Saturation Aesthetic in Indian Music, in: *Asian Music* XXXV, no. 1, fall/winter 2003/ 2004, pp. 115–134

Natarajan, Shobha : *'There are other ways to fuse East and West. Marry a European, eat their food. But leave Shastriya Sangeet alone!'* [Interview mit Ustad Vilyat Khan], in_*Sunday Observer* 15 April 1986

Nathan, J. : *Music of the Hindus*, in: Sourindo Mohun Tagore, *Hindu Music from Various Authors*, Varanasi 1965 [1875], pp. 213–232

Neuman, Daniel M. : *Saraswati's Changing Sound: An Anthropological Look at the Socio-Psychological Dynamics of Hindustani Music*, in: *Sangeet Natak* 34 (Oct-Dec 1974), pp. 81–86

The Social Organization of a Music Tradition: Hereditary Specialists in North India, in: *Ethnomusicology* 16/2 (May 1977), pp. 233–245

The Life of Music in North India. The Organization of an Artistic Tradition, Detroit 1990

Niranja, Tejaswini , Dhareshwar, P. Sudhir & Vivek : *Interrogating Modernity. Culture and Colonialism in India*, Calcutta 1993

Ord-Hume, Arthur W.J.G. : *Harmonium. The History of the Reed Organ and Its Makers*, New York 1986

Letter to the author dated 26 August 2003

Panikkar, K.N. : *Culture, Ideology, Hegemony. Intellectuals and Social Consciousness in Colonial India*, London [3]2001

Pasler, Jann : *India and its Music in the French Imagination before 1913*, in: S.A.K. Durga (ed.), *Music: Intercultural Aspects. A Collection of Essays*, Mumbai & Baroda 1999

Pingle, Bhavanrav A. : *Indian Music*, Delhi 1989 (first edition Kathiawar 1898)

Popley, Herbert A. : *The Music of India*, Delhi 1921, 1971

Powers, Harold S. : *Indian Music and the English Language: A Review Essay*, in: *Ethnomusicology* IX/1 (January 1965), pp. 1–12

Powell, Avril Ann : *Muslims & Missionaries in Pre-Mutiny India*, Richmond 1993

Prasad, Babu Nanak : *Indian Music. Scientific and Practical. Its Origin, History and Divisions; Writers of Old and Modern Times; Description and Classification of Ragas and Ragnis, Meanings and Museums of Tals and Suis; Forms and uses of Musical Instruments, Rulers of Playing on Sitar and Harmonium; Dissertation on Voice, Symphony, Notation and Phases and c. with Notes on Books and Professors of the Subject & c.*, first published in 1906; reprint New Delhi 2003

Purohit, Vinayak : Arts of Transitional India – Twentieth Century, Mumbai 1986

Quinet, Edgar : *Le Génie des religions*, in: *Œuvres complètes*, Paris 1857, pp. 55–74

Qureshi, Regula Burckhardt : *Sufi Music of India and Pakistan: Sound, Context and Meaning in Qawwali*, Chicago 1995 [1987]

Raju, S. Balachandra : *Learn Keyboard and Harmonium: Karnatic Music*, Chennai 1998

Ranade, Ashok Da : *Stage Music of Maharashtra*, Delhi 1986

Indology and Ethnomusicology. Contours of the Indo-British Relationship, Delhi 1992

Essays in Indian Ethnomusicology, Delhi 1998

Hindustani Music, Delhi 2002

Ratanjanker, S.N. : *Harmonium and Indian Music*, in: *Journal of the Sangeet Natak Akademi* 20 (1971), pp. 11–14

Redfield, Robert & Singer, Milton : *The Cultural Role of Cities*, reprinted in: Margret Redfield (ed.), *Human Nature and the Study of Society: The Papers of Robert Redfield* vol. 1 (1962), pp. 326–350

Rowell, Lewis : *Music and Musical Thought in Early India*, Chicago 1992

Roychaudhuri, Bimalakanta : *The Dictionary of Hindustani Classical Music*, Delhi 2000

Sangeet Natak Akademi: *Journal of the Sangeet Natak Akademi* 20 (1971), pp. 15–19 (AIR's Seminar on the Harmonium)

Sachs, Curt : *Die Musikinstrumente Indiens und Indonesiens*, Berlin 1923 [1914]

Said, Edward : *Orientalism*, New York et al. 1995

Culture and Imperialism, London 1994

Sangeet Natak Akademi: *Sangeet Natak Academy Bulletin. Rabindranath Tagore Centenary Number*, New Delhi 1961

Sangeet Research Academy: *Seminar on Sarangi. Organised by ITC-SRA (Western Region) 9th January 1994* [conference report], Mumbai, no date [1994]

Schwab, Raymond : *La renaissance orientale*, Paris 1950

Sengupta, Pradip Kumar : *Foundations of Indian Musicology. Perspectives in the Philosophy of Art and Culture*, Delhi 1991

Sharma, Amal Das : *Musicians of India, Past and Present. Gharanas of Hindustani Music and Genealogies*, Calcutta 1993

Sharman, Gopal : *Filigree in Sound. Form and Content in Indian Music*, Delhi 1970

Shankar, Ravi : *Hindustani Classical Music and the demands of today*, in: *Music East and West*, pp. 158–165

Singer, Milton : *When a Great Tradition Modernizes. An Anthropological Approach to Indian Civilization*, New York 1972

Singh, Thakur Jaideva : *Indian Music*, Calcutta 1995

Slawek, Stephen : *Keeping it going: Terms, Practices, and Processes of Improvisation in Hindustani Instrumental Music*, in: Bruno Nettl and Melinda Russell (eds.), *In the Course of Performance. Studies in the World of Musical Improvisation*, Chicago & London 1998, pp. 335–368

Solvyns, François Baltazard : *Les Hindôus, ou description de leurs moeurs, costumes, cérémonies...*, Paris 1810

Sorrell, Neil (with the late Gerry Farrell): *Colonialism, Philology, and Musical Ethnography in Nineteenth-Century India: The Case of S.W. Fallon*, in: *Music & Letters* 88 (1), February 2007

Sorrell, Neil & Narayan, Ram : *Indian music in performance: a practical introduction*, Manchester 1980

Spivak, Gayatri Chakravorty : *Can the Subaltern Speak?: Speculations on Widow Sacrifice*, in: *Wedge* 7 (8) (Winter/Spring) 1985, pp. 120–130

The Post-Colonial Critic. Interviews, Strategies, Dialogues, New York & London 1990

Srinivas, M.N. : *Social Change in Modern India*, Berkeley [5]1973 ([1]1966)

Stokes, Martin (ed.): *Ethnicity, Identity and Music. The Musical Construction of Place*, New York [2]1997

Strangways, A.H. Fox : *The Music of Hindostan*, Delhi 1994 (Oxford 1914)

Features, Principles and Technique of Indian Music, Delhi 1989

Subramaniam, P.V. : *The Harmonium in Light and Semi-Classical Music*, in: *Journal of the Sangeet Natak Akademi* 20 (1971), pp. 7–10

Tagore, Rabindranath : *Reminiscences*, in: *Sangeet Natak Academy Bulletin. Rabindranath Tagore Centenary Number*, Delhi [1961]

Handwritten letter to Dwarkin & Co., Kolkata. From the archive of Dwarkin & Co. [1888]

Gora, Calcutta 1951 [first published 1910]

Tagore, Sourindo Mohun : *Hindu Music from Various Authors*, Varanasi 1965 [1875]

Universal History of Music, compiled from diverse sources, together with various original notes on Hindu music, Calcutta 1896

Veer, Peter van der : *Imperial Encounters. Religion and Modernity in India and Britain*, Princeton 2001

Vir, Ram Avtar : *Learn to play on harmonium*, New Delhi, no date

Theory of Indian Music, Delhi 1999

Wade, Bonnie C. : *Khyal: Creativity in Tradition*, Cambridge 1984

Wagner, Christoph: *Zur Rezeption und weltweiten Verbreitung der Handharmonikainstrumente*, in: Monika Lustig (ed.), *Harmonium und Handharmonika*, Blankenburg 2002, pp. 195–202

Willard, Augustus : *A Treatise on the Music of Hindoostan: Comprising a Detail of the Ancient Theory and Modern Practice*, Calcutta 1834

Willard's Treatise on the Music of Hindustan, in: *Journal of the Asiatic Society* 25, 1834.

Woodfield, Ian : *The Keyboard Recital in Oriental Diplomacy*, in: *Journal of the Royal Musical Association*, 115 (1990), pp. 33–62

Music of the Raj. A Social and Economic History of Music in Late Eighteenth-Century Anglo-Indian Society, Oxford 2000

Yajnik, R.K. : *The Indian Theatre. Its Origins And its Later Developments Under European influence*, London, no date [1933]